Ruthless King

Kiara Morgan

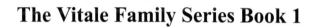

The Vitale Family Series Book 1

To all the dreamers

TABLE OF CONTENTS

CHAPTER 1

Anna

All my life I have been locked away in my own personal hell by my papa. To the outside world I'm a princess in designer clothes dripping in diamonds but what people don't see is the pain and scars hidden behind large iron gates and dozens of armed guards.

From a young age, I was told by my papa to be perfect, and anything less would result in pa punishment so severe that the thought of failing was worse than death.

I did my best to please my papa but was never good enough. I was reminded daily how little I was worth by my papa. As a female, I was considered an object that can only be traded to the highest bidder to benefit my father and the bratva.

The highest bidder who has won is the reigning Italian Mafia based in New York, The Vitale Family. I was told a few nights ago I was to marry the Capo of the Vitale Family to unite the family and increase our power.

My papa beamed at dinner at the thought of finally being able to expand our drug trades routes and thus increasing his power.

I push the long ivory curtains of my second-floor room windows and watch as the Vitale black SVU arrives. The first to exit is their driver who runs around the large vehicle in a haste and opens the backside door for a large man.

Right away I can tell he is Alessio Vitale, my soon-to-be husband. His immense presence can be felt all the way to my second-floor bedroom.

He is tall, has ruffled dark brown hair, brown eyes, a straight nose, and a chiseled square jaw.

At first glance, you would be captivated by his handsome face and muscled body, but behind that beautiful face, there is something dark lurking.

I have lived among monsters my entire life and I can easily recognize a monster hiding behind a clearly placed mask to hide one's true intentions.

Next to exit the vehicle is a man who is just as tall as Alessio but not as big. Both are attractive and look as though they work out, but Alessio is more buff whereas the second man is leaner.

From the dark brown hair and facial features, you can tell he is Alessio's brother. I know he has two brothers but I'm not sure which of the two he is.

The second oldest Vitale brother, Nico, is Alessio's right hand and consigliere. I know he is married and his wife is known to be a socialite who spends most of her time either shopping or partying.

Then there's the youngest brother, Carter. He is Alessio's and the Italian's enforcer.

From what I have heard he prefers to stay away from the business part of the mafia. I once heard my papa say he is a rabid dog who only knows how to kill. Based on that information, I would guess Nico was the one accompanying Alessio today since this meeting is related to business.

I should laugh at how ridiculous that sounds but the desolation that grips me can't find anything assuming about this situation. My marriage to Alessio is nothing more than a business deal.

The Vitale family is the controlling Italian Mafia family of not only New York but the entire east coast. They control several cities across the United States.

Alessio as their Capo has a reputation for being ruthless in his tactics and business dealings.

I've never met my soon to be future husband but have heard many rumors and stories. He had gained notoriety after his first wife and mother of his daughter Emma was killed by the Japanese Yakuza in a car bombing.

The target was rumored to have been Alessio but he wasn't there during the bombing.

After his wife was killed, Alessio slaughtered and dismantled the entire Yakuza from not only New York but the entire east coast in retaliation.

My papa and his associates were impressed at how brutally Alessio had handled the Yakuza. Which is probably why he was so eager to form an alliance with the Vitale Family.

It didn't matter to him that he was giving me, his only daughter, away to the same man he called merciless and cold.

I watch as they enter our home to meet with my papa, the Pakhan of Russian bratva.

My eyes begin to burn at the thought of my life being discussed without my knowledge or input. My father had decided every single factor of my life from the moment I was born till the next month when I'll turn eighteen years old when I will marry Alessio, who will then decide how I should live my life.

From one monster to another.

Alessio

My brother Nico and I entered the Petrov estate to discuss my marriage to Yuri Petrov's daughter, Anna. It's a large estate outside of New York City surrounded by large stone walls, and a state-of-the-art security system making it impossible for enemies to penetrate.

As soon as you walk in, there is a large painting of the Archangel Michael fighting demons hanging smack center of the wall in the foyer. Almost placed as a warning of the evil that resides within these walls.

The rest of the three-story mansion is full of large crystal chandeliers and white marble floors. The wealth drenched in the walls is apparent.

Yuri Petrov is not only the Pakhan of the Russian Bratva in New York but is CEO of Petrov Industries, a multi-billion-dollar shipping company. They have connections to top businesses and government officials around the world.

Despite those connections, they have been unable to expand towards the west, until now that is.

The thought of marrying a young girl who will be barely legal next month and is half my age revolts me but an alliance with the Petrovs is something we need.

The Irish had been trying to take control of our territory, while I was busy dealing with the Japanese Yakuza after they killed my wife. We have pushed back but the Irish won't sit idle for long and a war is inevitable.

They have been trying to increase their business into our territory for decades and have recently started closing in. With the number of resources and money spent handling the Yakuza, a war with the Irish would not only endanger my men but my family.

With Petrov's backing, it will push the war into our favor with the least number of casualties.

A man with short dark hair and grey eyes approaches. He is wearing a plain black t-shirt and has several tattoos covering both arms, and more peeking through from beneath his collar.

"I'm Dima, the Pakhan has been waiting. Follow me." He shows no emotions or reaction, as he guides us towards a hallway to the right, past two large staircases.

We get to two wooden doors with two guards standing outside. Dima nods at the guards and they open the door for us to enter.

Sitting behind a large wooden desk is Yuri Petrov, the Bratva Pakhan.

The large office has bookshelves going up to the ceiling with a large floor-to-ceiling window behind Yuri's desk. Yuri doesn't come off as a man who is into reading, my guess is that those books on the shelves are for display only.

From the corner of my eye, I notice Dima silently moving to one of the shadows of the room, almost becoming invisible.

Yuri smiles like a shark as he stands up to shake my hand. "Vitale, I'm glad to see you have decided to take up on my offer,"

Yuri has blonde hair with strands of grey mixed in, a long straight nose, and once blue eyes that have become cloudy with age.

"We need to discuss a few details before we finalize any deal." Despite the need for this alliance, the Petrovs have a reputation for being irrational and vicious. Getting the details of the alliance and other things outlined clearly will prevent any misperception.

Yuri frowns. "What exactly do we need to discuss? You marry my daughter and the Petrov family and the Vitale family will be united. In fact, you have more to gain from this alliance. You get a young bride and my family connections and resources."

I don't miss his tone or his suggestion that we need him more than he needs us. As much of a benefit it would be for the family, Yuri gains our drug trade routes not only within the city but the entire east coast.

The Petrovs have been trying to expand outside the city for years but have been unsuccessful. My marriage to Anna will benefit the Petrovs as much as it does my family.

I ignore Yuri's statement and continue with the most important reason for my visit today, Anna. "First of all, your daughter isn't even 18 years old yet."

Yuri waves his hand in the air as if that is of little importance, "She will be in one month."

"Second, I have yet to see her."

"You can see her at the wedding."

Nico glances at me; he was against this alliance from the beginning. Many rumors surround the Petrov family, none of which are good.

"I want to meet her before the wedding," I urge. I have yet to even see a picture of Anna. Yuri has kept her hidden from not only me but from the rest of the world too for the last several years. Over the years, there have been several rumors from Anna being disfigured due to an accident to being killed by Yuri in an act of rage. Considering this marriage proposal, we can cross off the latter.

Yuri sits back down behind his desk. "That's not possible, she is currently abroad. But she will return in time for the wedding."

I take a step forward towards Yuri, my anger surging at Yuri's refusal to show me his daughter. "How do you expect me to marry someone I have not yet met?"

"You are not marrying my daughter for her appearance but for her name and family." Yuri glares back.

He is right; it doesn't matter how she looks, but the secrecy of Anna's whereabouts does not sit well.

Aside from being my wife, she will also raise my daughter. I never intended this marriage to be anything but for business purposes and convenience. But I won't risk my daughter's safety by having an unfit teenager taking care of her.

"She will not only be my wife but the mother of my child. I have a three-year-old daughter, I need to know Anna is capable of taking care of her."

"She is capable," Yuri says with unconcern, "Besides if she's not I'm sure you can hire help for that."

Nico rolls his eyes at Yuri's remark of hiring help. He doesn't have children of his own but adores my daughter Emma. I could tell he has wanted children of his own but his self-centered wife Gia has refused, not wanting to ruin her body.

Yuri leans back on his chair. "If there is nothing else, should we move on to business?"

I have the desire to insist further but know I won't get anywhere. Yuri seems hell-bent on keeping Anna hidden until the wedding and at this point doesn't even matter.

This alliance is too valuable to break over the appearance of his daughter. I will just have to deal with her when I finally meet her.

We decide to move on and spend the rest of the time discussing the Irish, the trade routes, and how the alliance with the Petrov and the Vitale Family will form.

CHAPTER 2

Anna

I peek through the curtains and watch as the Vitale brothers and their driver get into their SVU.

Their meeting with my papa had lasted longer than I had thought. I wanted to sneak downstairs and listen in but if I had gotten caught, my papa would have skinned me alive.

He likes to keep me hidden in my own personal hell. I used to find solitude in my room away from papa and everyone else, but as I got older I resented being locked away.

I hear a knock at the door, and I go to open the door. It's Yulia, our long-time family maid.

She has been with my family since I was a child. I was raised mostly by my four older brothers and Yulia.

Despite having several nannies growing up, none stuck around long enough for me to even remember their names. Most of those nannies were too busy "taking care" of Papa. Yulia was the one constant I had.

"Your papa would like to see you," Yulia says with a thick Russian accent.

I know my papa wanting to see me is never a good thing. I take slow breaths to ease the nervousness forming in my stomach, "Okay, I'm coming," and follow her out.

I get to my papa's office and knock lightly. At first, I'm not sure if he has heard me but I don't want to knock any louder and upset him. Just as I am about to knock again, I hear him tell me to come in.

I walk into my papa's office and stand in the middle of the room. Not too far, but not too close. I know from my past several experiences what could happen if you are in reaching distance from him.

He looks up from his paperwork. "I just finished discussing the union with the Vitale family. You will marry next month once you turn 18. I also expect you to have Alessio's children right away. Since you are young, I'm sure getting pregnant within the first few months will not be an issue."

I'm surprised at my father's statement and how casually he mentions me having children. As if he's ordering food and not telling me, his still teenage daughter, to get pregnant.

I knew what is expected of me. I've prepared myself mentally since papa has told me of this union, but to have children so soon after my marriage is concerning.

"So quickly? I know Alessio has a child from his first marriage, I was hoping to get to know her before even thinking of having other children," I lightly say, hoping I don't offend Papa.

Truth is, I would rather not have children at all. I don't even know Alessio and can't even fathom having children with him. He might be my husband in a month but still a stranger.

My papa suddenly stands from his desk causing his chair to go flying into the wall behind him and storms towards me.

I start to back away in alarm, but he grabs me hard by my arm, cutting the blood circulation. I try to pull away but his grip only tightens further.

"You will be a good little daughter I raised you to be by marrying Alessio and then you will be a good wife and produce an heir to the Vitale Family. If I find out otherwise, even God can't save you. You will not ruin this for me!" he spits out.

I hurriedly nod at my father to please him, and he loosens his grip on my arm. "Now leave, I can't stand to see your damn face." He lets my arm go and looks at me with disgust.

I quickly run out of papa's office and continue to run towards my room. As much as I hate my papa and would love to go against him and make him pay a small fraction of the pain he has caused me by going against his orders, I know I never can.

The only ones who will get hurt are those that I love the most. He has a way of using the people I love as a tool to his advantage.

As I am about to turn the corner towards the stairs, I run into Ivan Levin and Sergai Kozlov, two of my father's associates and high-level bratva members.

Sergai blocks my path, preventing me from leaving, "Princess, I hear the Pakhan has sold you to the Italians."

I try to ignore him and go around but Sergai sticks his arm out preventing me from leaving.

He takes a step towards me and takes a piece of my hair and tucks it behind my ear, sending a shiver down my spine. "Such a pretty girl, I wish your papa just gave you to me as I asked."

I step away from Sergai in revulsion and he sneers at my retreat.

For years Sergai has watched me and would take every opportunity he could to get close to me.

Once during a Christmas Party, Sergai got drunk and put his hand on my thigh. My brother Damien threatened to cut off his hand when he found out.

Since then, I've always kept my distance from Sergai, and with my brothers around Sergai was never able to get close.

Now with them gone he takes every chance he can get and there is no one to stop him.

Sergai takes another step forward and I take one back, this repeats for a couple of steps until my back hits the wall.

I look at Ivan and hopelessly believe he might help me for once but he just stands there watching. Always watching. That's what Ivan does. Watch and gain information for his own advantage.

Ivan is in his mid-thirties, and the Obshchak, which is the bookkeeper for the bratva. He has dark brown hair, hazel eyes, and high chiseled cheekbones.

When I was young, I had a huge crush on him and would dream of marrying him when I grew up but now, I know better.

I was a fool back then who believed in fairy tales and happy endings.

For years I had hoped my prince charming would come and save me but a few years ago I finally realised the truth. No prince was ever going to come to save me, let alone Ivan.

He betrayed me in the worst possible way two years ago. I know now I am on my own.

Sergai however is the opposite of Ivan with his stubby appearance and greasy black hair. His deep wrinkles around his eyes and shallow cheeks show his age.

My father and Sergai have been friends for decades and he is my father's Sovietnik, his right-hand man.

Sergai leans forward, "I can help you Anna, just say you will be mine and I will get you out of this marriage with those Italian pigs," Sergai whispers into my ear. I can't help the tremor that runs down my spine from Sergai's close proximity. "Alessio is a monster who enjoys killing and torturing people. He will do the same to you. If you marry me, I will make sure you never have anything to worry your pretty little head about."

"Get away from me." I try to push him away, but he is stronger than me despite his age. All I do is exhaust myself.

My attempt to free myself makes Sergai laugh. "I love when my toys fight me."

Suddenly I hear a familiar male voice. "What's going on here?" I turn towards the voice and see it is Dima, the bratva enforcer.

Sergai steps away from me and gives Dima a wicked smile. "Just having a conversation, nothing for you to concern yourself with, Dima."

I take the opportunity to get away from Sergai, and I don't miss the smirk Ivan gives as I run past him.

I hate him of all people after his betrayal. He was someone I once trusted and believed to be my friend. He used my trust for his own advantage and didn't care about the pain he caused me.

Once I've safely reached my room and the door is locked, only then I let myself relax, and finally breathe.

I lean against my bedroom door but can't stop shaking. My body feels like it's vibrating at a high speed.

My eyes begin to sting, and tears endlessly fall down my face, one after another. I try to tell myself everything is going to be okay and to breathe in and out, but the pain in my chest is unbearable.

I fall to my knees and can't help but continue to cry at my life.

Alessio

We arrive at Encore, and I walk straight to my office on the second floor.

Encore is a nightclub and one of the many businesses owned by the Vitale family. The bottom floor has a large dance floor with two bars and the second floor has my office and our base of operations overlooking the entire club. The tinted mirror makes it appear as if it is a unique black wall instead of floor-to-ceiling windows that overlook the entire club.

As soon as I walk into my office, I notice my youngest brother Carter sitting in one of the chairs across from my desk with his phone in his hand.

"How was it?" Carter asks as he stands from his chair.

"Fine," I state flatly.

"It was not fine," Nico butts in, as he walks in behind me. "You can still back out, you know." Nico closes the door for the office.

I shake my head. "This alliance is important for the family and with the Irish making moves, it is even more imperative for this alliance to work."

"I can't believe you are willing to trap yourself and get married again," Nico huffs as he takes a seat on the leather couch across the room.

Nico married his wife Gia a month after I married my now deceased wife, Maria. Maria and Gia were best friends, but they were the complete opposite.

Maria was kind and caring, whereas Gia is a manipulative bitch.

The only reason Nico agreed to marry Gia was because she thought she was pregnant.

Turns out she wasn't, probably another one of her lies to manipulate Nico. She is always finding ways to get her way or make his life miserable and since we are Catholic, divorce is not an option.

"The deal is done and in a month I will marry Anna Petrov."

Nico shakes his head "It won't be that easy. You've heard the rumors about that family. Yuri's second wife killed herself to get away from that family. Not to mention Yuri's son Damien's death is still a mystery. Of course, let's also not forget about his sons, Nikolai who is in prison in Russia for murdering someone with his bare hands, Alek who is in a mental institution after setting a building on fire and killing 17 people for no reason, and last but not least Maxim. Who has been M.I.A. since he stabbed his pregnant girlfriend over a dozen times!" Nico shouts. "There's also Anna, who Yuri has kept locked away for two years and no one has seen since. What if the rumors about her being disfigured are true or something is actually wrong with her and that's why Yuri refuses to let you see her? What if she has a tail or something? Wouldn't be surprising considering she's a spawn of the devil."

I roll my eyes at Nico. Now he is just being dramatic.

Nico gets up and heads to the bar in the corner of the office and starts to make himself a drink. "You can still get out of this. We don't need the Russians or the Petrovs."

Nico's worries are valid. We are not saints but morally there are even limits we would not cross that the Petrovs don't have an issue with.

"I know this alliance isn't perfect, but we must make this work, especially with the threats coming from the Irish." I pause for a few seconds, "Also Emma needs a mother."

Nico pauses his drink midway at the mention of Emma. As much as Nico hates the idea of an alliance with the Petrovs, he knows I would do anything for Emma.

Last month on Mother's Day, Emma asked where her mother was, and I lied and told her she was on vacation. It broke my heart to see my precious daughter wonder where her mother is.

It is the first time she has ever asked but I have noticed her watching other children interacting with their mothers at family parties and gatherings.

Emma was only a few months old when Maria had died and I knew one day I would have to get re-married.

Maria was my friend before we married. We grew up together and when our families decided to arrange our marriage, I was pleased it was with someone I was comfortable with and knew. She knew what her responsibilities and obligations were and did them while I did mine. It may have not been the ideal marriage, but it worked.

After my failure to protect Maria, it prevented me from accepting previous offers from other families or high-ranking members within my own organization.

After Emma's inquiry, I decided it was time and the marriage offer came at the perfect time. Not only would Emma get a mother, but the family would benefit as well.

"Fine. If you want to marry a possibly disfigured girl who is half your age and get trapped in an ill-fated marriage, go ahead." Nico slams his drink onto the bar and storms out of the office, slamming the door shut as he leaves.

I turn to my brother Carter who looks completely uninterested by our complete interaction but that's not unusual for Carter. He never shows emotions, unless he is killing or torturing someone.

People call him stone cold, which is why he is such a good enforcer for the family.

I had hoped for Carter to be one of my underbosses, but he prefers to be an enforcer, stating it helps him relax.

Carter wasn't always like this. He used to be more carefree and had an easy-going personality, but now he rarely smiles unless he is teasing Nico but even then it is rare.

Three years ago, his girlfriend disappeared without a trace, around the same time my wife Maria had been killed.

People don't tend to just disappear without some evidence left behind.

But despite Carter searching for years, he could never find her or what happened to her.

Carter suspected for a while that the Yakuza had gotten to her but no one we questioned knew anything.

After that Carter went into a dark place and rarely showed any emotions outside the family.

"He will come around, he always does," Carter says as he tucks his phone in his pocket, "I have to go work."

I nod at Carter as he walks out.

I can't help but consider what Nico said could be true. This marriage could be doomed.

CHAPTER 3

One month later

Anna

A team of makeup artists and hairdressers complete their final touches on me.

My light blonde hair is pulled back into a chic bun and my makeup looks flawless but natural, emphasizing my blue eyes.

I look down at my wrist and start to fiddle with my gold bracelet with small snowflakes all around. It was a gift from my brother Damian before he died.

It doesn't match my dress, but I've never taken it off. It is a reminder of a happier time when I still had hope and dreams.

Yulia walks over to me and puts her hands on my shoulders. Her eyes turn teary as she looks at my reflection in the mirror.

"You look beautiful, just like your mama. You look so much like her."

My eyes start to sting at the mention of my mother. I never met her or know much about her.

She had jumped off the roof of our house when I was only a year old. She was around my age when she married my papa and I was told she couldn't stand to live with him anymore and took her own life. Leaving me behind with the man she hated so much she would rather die.

She was my papa's second wife after his first wife died of cancer. I heard my mother was a famous ballerina in Moscow and my papa had seen her at one of her performances and taken an interest. They married a few weeks after they met and less than a year later, she had given birth to me.

I clear my throat and turn to Yuila and stare at her warm face. She was hired by papa's first wife, the mother of my older brothers, as a maid and has been with the family since.

The thought of parting from her is unbearable. She is all I have now. I have no friends or other family around.

I try to hold in my tears, but a stray tear falls down my cheek. "Yulia, I don't think I can do this."

Yulia quickly pulls out a tissue from inside her purse and begins to wipe away my tears. "I know you can, you are stronger than you look. Now don't cry, you are going to ruin your makeup."

I look down at my hands. "I'm scared."

Yulia discards the tissue and holds my hands gently into hers. She smiles tenderly down at me. "Everything is going to be okay." She hesitates for a second then leans forward and whispers, "It's only for a few more months and then your brother Nikolai will be out of prison and he will help you, I know it."

My oldest brother Nikolai would never have agreed to this marriage union, but I'm not sure he can help me once he's out.

He has been serving time in prison in Russia for the last several months for murder. Papa could have easily gotten him out with his connections but has refused, stating he needed to learn to control himself.

I think it had more to do with his fear of Nikolai than teaching my brother any lesson.

For the last several years I have suspected he was getting scared of Nikolai and my other brothers and what they are capable of.

When I was younger, Papa used to love to exert his power over us but as my brothers got older, they became harder to control.

Papa used to love beating my brothers down but over time they became immune to the pain and his beatings.

I, along with those within bratva, could see he feared the monsters he had created but couldn't let anyone know it as it would make him look weak.

Someone knocks on the door and Yulia walks towards the door to answer. She opens it slightly and peeks her head out. All I can hear is someone murmur something to her. She turns back around. "It's time to go, Anna."

I take a deep breath and run a hand down my wedding dress and get up from my chair.

I take one quick glance in the mirror of my reflection and take in every small detail. I look beautiful and I know it should be the happiest day of my life, but I don't feel it.

All I feel is loneliness and loss.

"Okay let's go." I pull down my veil and turn towards Yulia who guides me out.

Yulia leads me to the front of the church where Papa is waiting. He is checking the time on his watch, most likely irritated that we are behind schedule by 20 minutes and he has been kept waiting.

When he sees me, he gives me a big smile. At first glance, you would think he is a happy father on his daughter's wedding day, but I know better. It is all for show, the tick in his jaw shows his true emotion. Annoyance or anger, most likely both.

I get a small bit of joy having annoyed my father and there is nothing he can do about it. He can't go beating me outside a church with everyone inside or present a bloody bride to the Vitales.

He leans forward and gives me a mild kiss on my cheek. I flinch out of habit, which only causes my father's tick in his jaw to deepen.

He looks me up and down, analyzing each detail, probably trying to find an error or mistake until he finally lands on my face. He raises my veil and takes a peek and then places it back down. "You look perfect. As you should. Do not forget what is expected of you, Anna," he warns.

"I know, Papa," I say quietly.

I put my arm around Papa's and he guides me towards the church doors.

Once at the doors, the music begins, and we start to walk down the aisle. The large veil on my head makes it hard for me to see anything or anyone, so I keep my eyes to the ground. I focus on walking down without tripping over the long white lace gown.

Suddenly, we stop and everything and everyone goes silent. All I hear is my beating heart that feels like it's going to fly out of my chest, along with some quiet whispers from the guests behind me.

I know at that moment we have arrived at the front, and I can't help but shake at the inevitable. My veil is lifted over my head and Papa gives my hand over to my future husband Alessio Vitale.

Alessio

The day has finally come for me to marry Anna. Despite Nico's insistence we should hire a stripper and throw a party, I opted to have a small gathering with my brothers and close friends the night before.

I have no interest in partying at my age, and besides, this is not my first marriage. I did the whole bachelor party and everything that comes with it when I married Maria.

This marriage is only a business alliance and nothing more. Anna will be my wife in name only.

If it wasn't for Emma, I would have moved Anna to one of our other apartments owned by the family after the wedding. I doubt she would have minded, considering she knows me as well as I know her.

She most likely had zero say in this marriage, whereas I had the option to at least refuse.

The wedding music begins, and the double church doors open to Yuri walking down the aisle with his daughter Anna. I can't see her face, as it's covered in a ridiculously enormous veil, but I notice my soon-to-be wife's body right away.

Anna is wearing a white lace off the shoulder dress that hugs her every curve and flows out just below her small waist.

I notice some of the men sitting in the pews leering up and down at Anna's body and I get the urge to stab them in the eyes.

Nico jabs his elbow into my side and leans over. "At least she has a nice body."

I jab my elbow back into him hard enough to cause him to cough but not too hard for the guest to notice. Nico just chuckles under his breath. *Fucker.*

Last night in a drunk state he came up with a poem comparing marriage to death. It ended with something along the lines of, "Your wife will stab you in the back with a knife." But I have a feeling it had more to do with his marriage than mine.

Gia had called him over a dozen times and he sent each call straight to voicemail.

Yuri and Anna arrive at the front and Yuri lifts Anna's veil over her head revealing her face for the first time.

I'm taken aback at seeing not only is Anna not disfigured but is breathtakingly beautiful. She has bright blue eyes, light golden blonde hair, and full pouty pink lips.

Yuri turns to me and hands me Anna's hand. I notice a slight tremor in her hand at my touch when I grab hold of her.

The priest clears his throat and begins speaking.

While the priest is reading the rites, I notice my young wife's hand continues to shake in mine.

She shifts and from the corner of her eyes, she searches the guests in the pew. I can't help but wonder who she is searching for.

The priest continues, and we say our vows and he declares us husband and wife.

When it's time to kiss, my now young wife goes pale, and her eyes widen. I can sense the hesitation but I pull her towards me and lean forward and gently kiss her on the lips. Her lips are soft and plump and I can taste vanilla, most likely from her lip balm.

The guests begin to cheer and I take a step back from Anna who looks up at me in confusion.

Nico pats me from behind and laughs. "Congratulations brother, I guess the rumors about her weren't true after all."

Anna's body tenses up at the mention of her name and turns and looks at Nico and then at me. Great, she clearly heard Nico, which isn't a surprise considering how fucking loud he is.

I grab Anna's hand and start walking down the aisle towards the church exit. We reach outside to dozens of people congratulating us until we finally reach the limo. The driver holds the door open for Anna and she gently holds her dress up and gracefully climbs into the limo.

I walk around the limo and get on the other side. As soon as the door shuts, Anna turns to ice once again and faces the window looking out, not making eye contact.

I can sense the fear she has for me, but I don't understand why. I have not done anything to her to suggest she should be afraid of me.

In my line of business, I do a lot of horrible things, but I would never hurt my family, and as my wife, that includes Anna, even if it is in name only.

She has no reason to fear me.

CHAPTER 4

Anna

We drive in silence to the wedding reception that is being held at a luxury hotel in Manhattan. I can tell Alessio is annoyed about something, and I decide it is better to stay silent than to say the wrong thing and tick him off.

I have learned over the years it is better to stay silent and do as you're told than to speak and make things worse.

At the reception, everyone is drinking and having a blast. My father made sure to spend top dollar on the décor and food. It would be a beautiful party if it was not a nightmare for me.

I can barely get food down at the thought of what's to come once the night ends.

I look around the party and can't help but notice that not a single person I care about is here. I search the crowd for a familiar face, someone who cares for me, or anyone who remotely has any interest in me, but find none.

Yulia was only allowed at the wedding to help me get ready but not at the reception. I tried to look for her during the ceremony but she must have been in the back and couldn't find her.

Instead, I see Ivan flirting with one of the waitresses and Sergai near the bar laughing loudly like a hyena as he grabs another drink. I hope he chokes on his drink.

"Who are you searching for?" My body instantly turns to stone at Alessio's question, who is sitting beside me.

I clear my throat and slowly turn towards him. "No one."

"You're lying. I know it's not your father since he is sitting right in front of us. Who. Are. You. Looking. For?" He turns his large muscled body towards me and I try to read his face but have a hard time deciphering him.

I don't know how to answer him and I'm afraid to say the wrong thing and anger him. Telling him I miss my family and feel lonely doesn't seem like the right thing to say at your wedding.

"Well don't you two make a cute couple," says a female with a high-pitched voice. I turn towards the voice and see a tall brunette with overly done makeup and a skin-tight bright pink gown with the neckline way too low walking towards us.

I release an internal sigh of relief of being saved for now by this stranger.

"I'm Gia, Nico's wife," says the tall brunette.

I get up from my chair to greet her and am stunned at the strong scent of perfume that goes instantly up my nose.

"Hi, I'm –" I'm cut off before I can introduce myself.

"Alessio, I get that she's young, but she should at least know how to behave."

"Excuse me?" I'm thrown off at Gia's comment.

"Your job is to look pretty and be a silent little Russian doll you are taught to be. No need to try and introduce yourself. No one cares." She scoffs.

I know I should just keep quiet and not say anything, but I am tired of being stepped on by my papa and now I have to hear it from some stranger I just met.

"The thing about authentic Russian dolls is that there are a number of hidden dolls inside. You think you have it all figured out only to find out later there are countless secrets concealed inside. Don't underestimate a doll."

I turn to Alessio hoping he's not too upset at my insolence but notice his lips twitch slightly almost in amusement.

"I don't know what you're trying to imply, but you should know your place," Gia sneers.

"It is you that needs to know your place, Gia." Alessio stands from his chair and puts his arm around my waist and pulls me towards him, catching me off guard. "Anna is now my wife and as Capo, any disrespect towards her, I consider disrespect towards me. Do you understand?"

Gia opens and then closes her mouth like a fish for a few seconds. "I didn't mean to disrespect you, I'm... I'm sorry," She stammers and walks away but not before giving me a death glare.

I know this won't be the end of her. I make a mental note to keep an eye out for her next time.

I turn to Alessio. "I'm sorry, I didn't mean to cause any problems between you and your sister-in-law."

"You didn't. And no one should talk to you in that manner, family or not. You are my wife now. Remember that, Anna."

I take in his words, his wife. His wife, till death do us part.

Alessio

During our first dance, Anna pouted the entire time. As annoying as it was, it was also cute in a way.

She is young and I know I have to be patient with her. But she is completely closed off.

She was searching for someone earlier in the church and again here at the reception but won't tell me who.

She wears her emotions on her sleeve, which makes it easier for me to know how she feels but refuses to speak about them.

Once our dance ends, Anna excuses herself to go to the ladies' room.

Nico walks over to me. "Is the honeymoon phase already over? Having a lover's quarrel already?"

"Aside from your wife being a bitch to Anna, everything's fine."

"That is why I have been avoiding Gia the entire night, she has a way of making everyone around her miserable." Nico takes a sip of his drink.

"I need a drink too." A waiter walks towards our direction and has a drink ready in his hand. I instantly grab it and finish it in one go.

Carter comes to stand next to Nico. "I guess things aren't going well?"

I rub my forehead because of these two. "I'm ready to get back home."

"Ready for the real honeymoon to begin you mean." Nico nudges me with his elbow to my side. "But don't get too excited because it doesn't last long."

I roll my eyes. "I'm starting to get a headache because of you two and I'm ready for this night to end."

Anna walks out of the washroom and stops to look around again.

"Who is she looking for?" I can't help the annoyance forming.

"Maybe her boyfriend," Nico shrugs.

"Yuri would have mentioned that. He made it clear she was pure."

I remember the pitch Yuri presented, almost making it sound like he is selling me a piece of land rather than handing over his only daughter.

After searching the room Anna once again pouts in an adorable way, looking almost defeated. The thought of Anna searching for her boyfriend or even having a boyfriend riles me.

I know we just married and it's unreasonable for me to be upset but the thought of her pining for someone else enrages me for some reason.

"Have you seen her? She has every male's attention tonight. There is no way someone who looks like that hasn't been with a guy at some point," Nico states.

As much as I love Nico, I have the urge to punch him in the face right now.

"Either way, you will find out tonight if she is pure or not." Nico smirks above his glass.

I ignore Nico and walk towards Anna before I hit my own brother in the face.

When her eyes meet mine, they widen slightly.

"We're leaving, do you want to say goodbye to your family?" I ask Anna.

She looks down at her wrist and starts to play with a gold bracelet she is wearing. She sighs and quietly mumbles, "No."

"Let's go then." I put my hand on her lower back to lead her out and she flinches at my touch but follows my lead.

I lead Anna out of the party and a number of drunk guests get up and cheer.

CHAPTER 5

Anna

We get to Alessio's penthouse and take the exclusive elevator to the top floor.

I notice Alessio rubbing his forehead with his thumb and forefinger.

During the car ride, he had taken a painkiller due to most likely a headache from the long day we had.

I'm exhausted mentally and physically from today.

I had been woken up before dawn to start getting ready. I'm sure Alessio must've woken up at the same time considering all the preparation needed to be done before the ceremony. He is also Capo so he must have had to finish his work before the wedding.

We arrived at the top floor and the elevator doors swing wide open and we entered straight into the penthouse.

I glance around my new surroundings and home, but it is too dark to make anything out.

I can see a glimmer of city lights from behind long curtains, in what I am assuming is the living room with the lights off but can't make out much of anything else.

"The staff will show you around properly tomorrow morning," Alessio murmurs, as he begins loosening his bow tie. "I'll show you to our room."

He starts walking towards a set of stairs and I silently follow him. With each step I take, my heart thumps louder.

We reach a door at the end of the hall, and I know we have reached Alessio's bedroom. Our bedroom now. He opens the door and gestures for me to go in. I hesitate first but then decide to go in, knowing I have nowhere else to go.

I step inside and take in the large bedroom. My heart feels as though it's about to fly out of my chest at an uncontrollable speed.

I hear the door shut behind me and I can't help but jump in fright.

Alessio frowns at my reaction. "Relax, I'm not going to hurt you or touch you if you don't want me to."

That eases my mind but I know if we don't consummate this marriage, Papa will have my head. "I know what is required of my duty."

Alessio's frown deepens. "I don't care for your duty. If you want to change and go to sleep, we can discuss this tomorrow morning."

I shake my head. "No, we need to consummate this marriage."

Alessio looks surprised at my statement, but I can't disappoint Papa. Who knows what he will do if I fail at making this marriage work?

Papa has reminded me since I was little my only value was to be a good wife and mother. Unlike my brothers who could be soldiers and leaders within the bratva, I was of no real use.

Women are considered weak and useless to the bratva.

Alessio nods and takes a step forward towards me, and I force myself mentally not to move or react. He goes around me and starts to unbutton my dress but despite my attempts, I can't stop my body from trembling.

"This isn't going to work," Alessio sighs and steps back.

"I'll be fine."

He shakes his head. "Maybe you need something to calm down."

He walks over to the table near the window and picks up a bottle of champagne. He pops it open and pours it into two glasses and hands me one.

I take the glass and take a sip and scrunch my nose at the bitter taste.

Alessio chuckles at my reaction. "You don't like champagne?"

"Never had it before. I'm eighteen, remember?"

Now Alessio scrunches his nose at my mention of my age. "Did your dad not even let you drink for parties or special occasions?"

"My papa didn't have a problem with it, it was my brothers who didn't want me drinking." My heart hurts at the mention of my brothers. I take another sip.

The taste gets better with each sip. Once the glass is empty, I start to feel my nerves loosen and almost on a high.

No wonder my brothers loved to go out and drink, especially on those difficult days at work.

Alessio grabs my glass and puts both glasses down on the table. "I'm going to help you with your dress, okay?"

I nod my head and turn around to give him access to the zipper on the back.

He pulls the zipper down my back and starts pulling the dress down. I help by shimming out and kneeling forward to step out of the giant lace pile in front of me when my butt clashes with Alessio's legs when I kneel forward. He made a strange noise in his throat which startles me.

I step out of my dress and now I'm standing with only my lace white bra, matching undies, and heels in the center of the room. I kick off my heels to the side and I look to Alessio for guidance as my nerves are slowly creeping up on me again.

"Lay down on the bed," Alessio almost growls.

I take a step towards the bed but remember the pins in my hair. I quickly pull them out, letting my long blonde hair fall down my back in loose curls.

I then crawl onto the center of the bed and lay on my back, unsure of what to do.

I hear some rustling and look up to see Alessio remove his shirt. He reminds me of a bronzed god with all the muscle. He tosses his shirt to the side and removes his shoes and begin to unbuckle his belt. He tosses his pants to the side with his shirt and shoes and is left with only his black boxer briefs.

Alessio comes and kneels over me. "Are you sure about this?"

I give him a quick nod.

He slides out of his boxer briefs and the first thing I notice is his cock. His enormous cock.

"Oh my god!" I squeal unintentionally and feel my face going red by the second.

Alessio's lip twitches. "Are you ready?"

"Yes." The truth is I'm not ready but I don't think I ever would be.

Alessio climbs on top of me, parts my legs, and guides his cock to my opening, but I can't help but shrink back.

"Anna," he says pleadingly.

"Sorry, can you just hold me?" I ask hopingly. At least I won't be able to move.

He looks at me with confusion and then puts his arm around my waist and pulls me closer to him. "Like this?"

I nod. "Yes."

I am inches away from Alessio and can feel his body heat radiating towards me. But for some reason, I feel more at ease this way.

Alessio shifts his hips so his tip nudges my entrance. He slowly pushes in a bit. I clench at the intrusion and grip his biceps for support. He pushes in completely, and my body shudders in pain.

"Are you okay?" His voice is laced with concern.

I give a small reassuring smile. "I'm fine."

Alessio looks at me and once he finds the answer he was looking for, he begins to thrust into me with shallow, gentle thrusts.

Each time he pumps into me, I feel a mix of pain and slight pleasure that starts to increase with time.

After a while, the thrusts become harder, and then he tenses with a sharp exhale. I, too, freeze at the feeling of utter fullness, not sure if I was going to come apart at the seams or if my body was falling off a cliff into a pile of tingling ecstasy.

I feel him release deep inside of me. After the high comes down, Alessio slumps on top of me as we both try to get our breathing under control.

He gets up on his elbows and looks at me with such warm eyes and then all of sudden I see a shift.

As if darkness has clouded his eyes and he looks at me with confusion, almost as if he doesn't recognize me.

"Alessio." I cautiously put my hand on his cheek lightly.

At first his eyes become warm and then like a viper attacking his prey, he grabs me by my neck. I recoil and try to back away, but his hold tightens around my neck.

"Alessio," I beg but it's no use. His grasp squeezes around my neck and I'm rattling for air.

My body trembles to get oxygen. I scratch his hands to try and have him release me, but I can feel myself losing consciousness.

I start to see colorful dots and then everything goes black.

CHAPTER 6

Alessio

I wake up to a pounding headache and look to the left and see on the nightstand the clock says 4:00 am in bright red writing.

I had a horrible nightmare where I had dreamed of Maria but a mutated version of her after the bombing. She was trying to kill me for failing to protect her.

I had similar dreams in the past when Maria was first killed but this is the first time it had felt real.

I turn to my right and see Anna lying motionless beside me. The memories of last night come rushing back to me like a tsunami at the sight of Anna.

I remember coming back to the penthouse with Anna but that's when things got hazy.

There are dark ghastly purple marks around Anna's neck.

In my dream, I had choked Maria to stop her, but I realise now it wasn't a dream. It was Anna who I had choked.

I quickly get up and feel for a pulse to make sure she is breathing. Once I feel a pulse, I can't help the wave of relief that flows down my body.

How could I let this happen? I could have killed Anna last night.

It wasn't a dream but hallucinations I saw last night. Most likely due to a drug, which would also explain the hammering headache I have right now.

I try to think back to when I could have ingested it. It had to be at the reception party.

The food was prepared by the staff who we had thoroughly vetted but someone could have sneaked in.

I lightly trace the bruises on my young wife's neck and feel a sharp pain in my chest.

I look over Anna's body to make sure I didn't hurt her anywhere else. When I reach her legs, I notice the pink between her legs.

I am truly a monster. No wonder she was afraid of me.

I head to the washroom and shut the door behind me and slump against it trying to get my emotions in control.

I lost control and hurt Anna in the worst way possible.

I grab a small towel and wet it and head back to the bedroom and gently wipe between her legs. Once I have cleaned her up, I cover her up with a blanket and discard the towel in the bathroom.

I quickly change and decide to head to Encore to figure out what happened.

As I leave the room, I turn around and see Anna lying unmoving in bed, with her golden blonde hair splayed across the pillow.

She looks almost angelic if not for my tainted marks on her neck.

Nico was right, this marriage was doomed, and I am to blame for this.

Anna

I wake up to the sun hitting my face from the open curtains. I look around the room and don't recognize it.

Instantly memories of last night come back to me. My hand goes straight to my neck and a cold shiver runs down my spine.

Alessio choked me.

I look around the room and don't see him. Tears fall down my cheek and I wipe them away quickly.

I can't break now, I tell myself. I've survived worse, I will survive this too.

I get up and walk into the bathroom and stand in front of the mirror.

The bruising around my neck is now a horrible shade of purple. My eyes are puffy and red and my cheeks are blotchy from crying.

I should be used to seeing myself like this, after all, Papa has done worse, but the thought I went from one hell to another is unbearable.

More tears fall down my cheek and my chest feels tight as if it's going to explode from the pain into tiny little pieces.

I hold on to the counter and tell myself over and over again I will be okay.

After thirty minutes I can finally breathe normally again. I decide to take a quick shower to clean myself up and then finish doing my morning routine. I pop my head out of the bathroom and listen for Alessio but find it quiet.

I head over to the walk-in closet and see that my clothes are already placed in the closet.

Of course, my clothes have been placed in the closet. This is my new home, my new prison now, and I need to get used to that.

I skim through my wardrobe and decide on a simple light blue summer dress. I put on a neutral-colored lipstick, add some mascara and finish my look with a pair of strappy heels.

My hair is now dried and flowing down my back in waves.

I stand in front of the mirror and try to find any flaws in my appearance.

I notice the bruises on my neck and grab a bottle of makeup concealer and cover up the bruises. It takes a couple of layers but it's almost unnoticeable. As long as no one looks right at them or comes too close, no one will know.

I walk downstairs to the first floor and I'm now able to get a better look at the penthouse in the daylight.

The floors are dark wood and there is floor to ceiling windows in every room, giving a beautiful view of New York City.

Despite living so close to the city, my family has always lived outside of the city for privacy. The only view I ever saw from my window was of the estate grounds that went on for miles.

I walk over to one of the windows and stare out at the city.

I can't help but press against the window as I take in the view. Everyone below looks like ants from up here.

Someone clears their throat behind me, and I quickly turn around in a jolt.

Standing in front of me is a plump woman possibly in her mid-fifties. She is wearing a simple black dress with her hair pinned in a chignon.

"Hello, my name is Greta, I am the main housekeeper. It's a pleasure to meet you, Mrs. Vitale."

I cringe at her calling me Mrs. Vitale and notice her brows furrow at my reaction.

I give her a smile. "It's nice to meet you as well. You can call me Anna."

She looks unsure at first at my request to be called by my name but gives me a warm smile that reminds me of Yulia.

"Let me show you around, Anna. This is the living room of course, and the room on the left of me is the dining room." Greta motions for me to follow her. I smile at her, as she leads me down the hallway.

"Here we have the kitchen and further down the hallway is Mr. Vitale's office."

"Is Alessio in his office?" I get an uneasiness in my stomach at the thought of seeing him.

"No, he usually doesn't work from home." Greta walks into the kitchen and I follow behind her like a lost lamb.

The kitchen is all marble and stainless steel. One wall of the kitchen is all glass, similar to the windows in the living room. I used to cook and bake with Yulia. I wonder if Greta would mind if I used the kitchen occasionally.

"Why don't you take a seat at the table and I will grab a plate of breakfast for you?"

"I can make my own plate." I go to grab the plate out of Greta's hand but she gently nudges me towards the table. I decide to do as I'm told and take a seat at the large kitchen table.

A few minutes later, Greta puts a plate of scrambled eggs, toast, and fruit in front of me.

I quietly eat my breakfast alone at the table and can't help but feel sad. At home, I had the guards, Dima, and Yulia but here I have no one.

Greta seems nice and reminds me of Yulia, but it is not the same.

I finish eating my breakfast and stand to put my dishes away when Greta comes over and grabs my dishes from my hand.

"I can put my own dirty dishes away." I try to grab the plate back but Greta shakes her head.

"You are married to the boss, it is my job to do this."

I want to argue but know it's pointless.

Greta finishes filling up the dishwasher and turns towards me. "Are you ready to meet Emma?"

I freeze on the spot at the mention of Emma. How could I forget about Emma, Alessio's three-year-old daughter? I was so worried about seeing Alessio, I forgot about Emma.

I nod at Greta and follow her upstairs to a room I passed by this morning on my way downstairs.

Greta opens the door and we walk into a large room, with a white bed and light pink bed sheets with dolls scattered around the floor as if a toy explosion had gone off.

In the middle of the scattered doll mess is a small girl with dark brown hair and large brown eyes, playing with a doll.

She looks up at me and then at Greta and looks confused at first.

Greta clears her throat. "Emma, I want you to meet your mother."

I halt at Greta calling me Emma's mother. I knew Alessio expected me to raise Emma but being called her mother, I didn't expect. Emma had a mother and I know I can never take her place.

Suddenly Emma gets up and walks towards me and my heart starts racing at seeing this little girl standing in front of me and I'm not sure what to do or say to her.

At first, she looks mystified but then Emma slowly smiles and drops her doll on the ground and wraps her arms around my legs.

"I've been waiting for you," she whispers into my dress. I gently stroke her hair and smile down at Emma. She lets go of my legs and grabs my hand. "Come Mama, play with me." She drags me to a small table in the corner. "Can we have a tea party?" Emma asks with her large chocolate brown eyes.

I can't help the permanent smile that's etched onto my face and nod. "Of course. Let's have a tea party."

Emma beams and quickly sits down in the small chair and I follow her lead and sit down in the other small chair. She starts pouring imaginary tea in a teacup and I hear the door behind me close. I turn to see Greta has left and now it is just me and Emma.

"Here Mama!" Emma hands me a small toy teacup and I can't help but beam back at her.

The sadness I felt only a few minutes ago is now gone and replaced with joy.

Alessio

I am finishing up reading some financial reports when Nico barges into my office with a huff. He slams the door shut behind him with such force it causes the entire room to vibrate.

"I could kill Gia!" Nico slumps into the chair in front of my desk with a loud thud.

I should have known Gia was behind Nico's sudden irate behavior. She has a way of pushing my brother's buttons. I sense she gets enjoyment out of making him miserable considering how often she does it.

"What did Gia do now?"

"She fired Lucy because she didn't make her tea hot enough," Nico seethes.

Lucy is Nico and Gia's latest housekeeper. Gia has a habit of firing the staff after a couple of weeks for one reason or another. The last housekeeper was fired because she didn't like the shoes she wore to work.

"Fuck, why can't I just strangle her to death," Nico groans back into the chair.

"It wouldn't look good for us to be killing our own wives." Even though I almost killed my own wife only a few hours ago.

"Then I guess I just have to find a way to make her life hell the way she makes mine," Nico says smugly.

"And how do you plan on doing that?"

Nico straightens in his chair. "Well first I won't hire any more help." Nico slowly smiles. "She will hate that she has to clean up after herself for once. That will teach her a lesson."

My office door swings open yet again, and Carter walks in. "You're here early considering it is the day after your wedding."

Nico stops smiling. "Wait, why are you here? Is the honeymoon already over?"

I shake my head at the thoughts from the wedding night. "Something like that."

"I knew this marriage was destined to fail from the start." Nico raises to his feet and crosses his arms. "Don't tell me Anna is another Gia? A monster in disguise."

Nico comparing Anna to Gia causes a wave of unexpected anger within me.

I slam my laptop shut and look up to see Nico and Carter standing still due to my sudden reaction.

I sigh. "Anna is nothing like Gia, in fact, the monster is me." Nico and Carter look surprised at my statement. "Someone drugged me last night, I need you two to find out who."

Nico's eyebrows shoot up. "What do you mean you were drugged?"

"Last night I started to have hallucinations. It had to be someone at the reception. That is the only place I could think of where I could have consumed something without my knowledge."

I can tell my brothers have questions, but they don't ask.

Carter steps forward. "I'll look into it and let you know anything I find out."

"I knew this was not a good idea." Nico shakes his head.

After Carter and Nico leave, I continue to work but my mind keeps wandering back to Anna and her still body this morning.

She looked so small and broken and I am to blame for that. I inflicted pain on my own wife. I wonder if she is okay or in pain.

If she wasn't, I know Greta would have informed me by now. She had messaged me earlier to let me know everything is going well.

But I can't help but wonder what she is doing and how she is feeling. I get up from my desk and decide to head home and check in on Anna. I quickly text my driver to meet me in front of the building.

Once I exit the building, my driver is waiting and opens the door to the SUV. Within a few minutes, we arrive back at my penthouse and I take the elevator straight up to my floor.

I can't help but feel nervous. I haven't felt this nervous since I was a teenager.

I always make sure to plan my every move to ensure I am always in control and for once I have lost control.

The elevator doors dings open and I find it quiet.

I head over to the kitchen and find Greta cooking away. She seems to be making some sort of pasta from the smell and large pan on the stove.

She looks up and startles at seeing me, "God!" Greta holds a hand to her chest and breathes heavily in and out. "I'm sorry, I was unaware you were going to be returning home early tonight."

"Where is Anna?"

"Upstairs with Emma."

Emma. I hadn't planned on Anna meeting Emma so soon. I should have messaged Greta earlier and informed her to keep Emma away until I was able to make sure Anna was capable of taking care of my daughter. With the events of last night, I had overlooked this.

I head upstairs to the bedrooms and as I near Emma's bedroom I hear giggles from the other side of her door.

I approach quietly and see Anna sitting at Emma's small table set drinking from a small teacup.

Her long blonde hair cascades down her back in waves. She gently pats Emma's head as she finishes drinking from her teacup.

"Mommy, have some more!" Emma beams as she pours imaginary tea from her teapot into Anna's teacup.

My heart melts at seeing Emma so happy but I can't help but be on alert at Emma calling Anna mom. I had planned on Anna to raise Emma and be a mother to her but to hear it out loud from my child's mouth sets it in stone.

My phone rings suddenly and Anna spins from her seat and our eyes lock. Her face goes pale and her eyes widen from shock and terror.

"Daddy, you're home!" Emma runs out of her small chair and runs towards me at lightning speed.

I crouch down to her level. "I have some work to do, but I'll be back later."

"It's okay, I have Mommy now." Emma runs back to her chair and starts fidgeting with her tea set once again.

But Anna continues to sit frozen in the small chair watching, almost waiting. Probably thinking I will choke or kill her right there.

I take a look at my phone and see it's a text message from Nico asking to meet him at Carter's. As I turn to head out, I notice from the corner of my eye Anna sigh in relief at me leaving.

I wonder if this is how it's going to be from now on? Anna fearing me every time I am near.

I can't blame her, but I can't have her living in fear either.

CHAPTER 7

Alessio

I take the elevator down two floors to Carter's penthouse. The top three floors of the building belong to my brothers and me. We all share the same private elevator giving us access to each other's penthouse. Mine is at the top, while Nico and Gia's are below us and Carter's the third last.

Nico tends to spend most of his time at Carter's to avoid Gia but I think also to secretly keep an eye on Carter.

Carter would never admit it, but since his girlfriend's disappearance, he has lived in darkness. Sometimes Nico and I fear that the darkness will one day consume him and take him from us.

Once I reach Carter's floor and step out of the elevator, I find Nico and Carter in the living room.

Nico turns towards me. "We have some good news and some bad news. We know who drugged you, but we can't prove it."

"What does that mean?"

"We went over the security footage at the hotel and found a waiter had put something in your drink."

"We found the waiter and after some persuading," Carter tilts his head to the side, "We were able to get him to talk."

Meaning Carter had to torture the guy. If some waiter thought he could drug me and get away with it, he's either a fool or an idiot or maybe both.

"He admitted Ivan Levin hired him to give you the drugged drink but," Nico trails off, "he jumped off the fourth floor of his apartment window when we weren't looking."

Fuck! Without any proof, we can't go after Ivan or make a move against the bratva.

They would consider it an unprovoked attack and would start a war between the two families. This union was meant to strengthen our family, not destroy it.

Carter leans against the wall. "The waiter is currently in a coma and we have someone monitoring the situation and will let us know when he wakes."

We can't wait for the waiter to wake up and even if he does, who's to say his memory wouldn't have been damaged.

I consider our options for a second and come to the conclusion that I can't move against Ivan. It is too risky but that doesn't mean I'll let him off the hook.

I turn to Nico. "Set up a meeting with Ivan."

"I'll do that, but we can't let him get away with this. He dared to make a move against the Vitale family by drugging the Capo." Nico shakes his head, "These fuckers need to be taught a lesson."

"You know we can't make a move against Ivan without proof. Even making an accusation without proof can break the alliance between us and the Petrovs."

"Fuck the Petrovs!" Nico shouts, "They tried to drug you."

Nico has a point, if any other family tried to do this, we would have attacked them by now but we can't afford a war with the Russians and the Irish at the same time.

"We will take care of Ivan another way, without causing a war between the two families."

Nico nods and I can tell he wants to say something but holds it in. Which I'm thankful for as I can't be fighting with my brothers as well.

"I'm going to head back up, Nico, are you going to head home?"

Nico scoffs at my mention of him heading to his own place and takes a seat on the couch. "Not right now. I think I'm going to stick around here with Carter and watch the game."

Carter rolls his eyes and Nico makes himself comfortable on the couch.

I'm surprised Nico hasn't already moved into Carter's penthouse permanently.

He and Gia barely spend any time together unless it's for events or family functions that require them both to make an appearance.

At first, they were able to pretend to be a happy couple but eventually, Nico got tired of it and now barely shows restraint in public when out with Gia.

I'm about to head back up when Carter comes back from the kitchen with two beers. "Why don't you stay as well?"

"He probably wants to get back to his new young wife," Nico says as he stretches out his arms above his head and leans back into the couch with his feet crossed on the coffee table.

Carter kicks Nico's legs off his table. "Not everyone wants to avoid their wives like you, Nico."

Nico glares at Carter. "Whatever." He grabs a beer out of Carter's hand.

Carter shakes his head at Nico and turns around and hands me a beer. I pause but then take it from him as Carter heads back to the kitchen to grab himself one.

"I guess I can stay for a bit." I sit down at the end of one of the couches and take a large chug of the beer.

After seeing Anna with Emma and her reaction to me, I don't know how to handle the situation.

She seems to be doing well with Emma but clearly fears me. If I tell her I was drugged, would that change anything? I still hurt her and caused her pain. She might not even believe me.

I take another large drink of the beer and Carter comes to sit next to Nico with his own beer in his hand.

Nico laughs. "I guess all men do want to avoid their wives after all." He elbows Carter in the side, causing Carter to again roll his eyes.

Nico is not entirely wrong. I am avoiding Anna.

Anna

After Alessio's sudden appearance and just as quick disappearance, the rest of the day is spent playing different games with Emma.

For dinner, Greta cooked an amazing meal and despite only being me and Emma, we had a great time.

After dinner, I bathed Emma and got her ready for bed. I tucked her into bed and grabbed a book from her bookshelf and read her a bedtime story.

Halfway through the book Emma fell asleep and I couldn't help but smile as she cuddled into my side. I wanted to stay and sleep the night there, but I had to face Alessio eventually.

I closed Emma's door gently and went back to my bedroom I now share with my husband who I barely know.

To my surprise, Alessio wasn't there. I quickly finished my bedtime routine and changed into a silver silk camisole with lace detailing around the neckline and matching shorts.

My eyes land on my neck in the mirror once again. The bruising has darkened throughout the day and looks worse than ever.

I wish I had some sleepwear that covered more but papa had asked a stylist to pack my wardrobe and to throw out anything not fitting for a wife.

My eyes start to feel heavy, and I decide to call it a night and go to sleep. I should be concerned about my husband not being home yet but I'm not.

For all I know he is working or with a mistress. The thought of Alessio having a mistress makes me feel relieved rather than angry. I wouldn't mind if he would rather spend all his time with a mistress than here with me.

I shut off the lights and crawl into bed and within minutes the darkness consumes me, and I fall asleep.

So much blood. I can't see anything but blood. My eyes are blurry from tears, but I try to crawl forward, but I am grabbed by my hair and pulled back.

"Please! Please don't do this! I'm begging you!" I scream in pain. The pain is too much. It hurts and I can't breathe. I try to fight but it's no use, I am too weak, I have always been weak. But I can't stop fighting. I try to break free but I'm being held back.

I wake to find Alessio hovering above me. He looks shocked and it takes me a second to realize I was having a nightmare.

"Anna, are you okay?" His voice is laced with concern.

I breathe in and out to try and calm myself and tell myself it's okay. After a few seconds, I realize Alessio's hands are on my shoulders, and out of instinct I push his arms away and pull away from him.

He looks almost hurt at first but quickly masks it to indifference so quickly you wouldn't have even noticed it if you blinked.

"You were crying in your sleep," he says emotionlessly.

"I'm fine."

We stare at each other for a few seconds, and he nods and heads towards the bathroom. I hear the shower turn on a few seconds later.

I try to go back to sleep but every time I close my eyes, I see blood. A few minutes later the shower turns off and Alessio walks out with only a towel around his waist.

I close my eyes and try to even out my breathing, hoping he believes I'm asleep.

A few seconds later the mattress dips and I can feel the warmth from Alessio beside me.

He doesn't move or say anything for a while and I hope he's asleep but I know better.

After what feels like hours of me pretending to sleep, my eyelids start to get heavy, and I finally drift off to sleep.

CHAPTER 8

Alessio

Anna pretended to be asleep when I came out of the bathroom but as soon as I got into bed her body instantly went rigid. Eventually, she fell asleep but I, on the other hand, had a harder time falling asleep.

Even in darkness, the bruises around Anna's neck were visible from the moonlight coming through the windows. I couldn't stop staring at them throughout the night.

I have done worse damage to my enemies but seeing those marks on Anna almost felt as though they were taunting me. How I have failed for the second time as a husband to protect my own wife. The first due to my enemies and this time due to my own actions.

My driver pulls the SUV next to Nico and Carter's cars. "Stay here and wait for me. I will let you know when I'm ready to leave." My driver nods his head as I exit the vehicle.

I meet Nico and Carter inside the warehouse that is now nothing but an empty space with random pieces of wood and broken crates scattered around.

Nico puts his phone into his jacket pocket. "Ivan will be here soon. It's still not too late to kill that fucker."

I shake my head. "Why did I make you my consigliere again?"

"Because I'm good at dealing with people. And this one here refused to deal with people unless it involved killing them." Nico motions towards Carter who is leaning against the wall, clearly unhappy about being here.

A car pulls up and Ivan gets out with two guards. "Remember, no killing," I warn Nico.

"What is the reason for this meeting?" Ivan removes his sunglasses and tucks them into his jacket. "If you are unhappy with Anna, you should take that up with Yuri."

I get the urge to kill him despite telling my brother only twenty seconds ago the contrary.

Nico glares at Ivan. "You know exactly why we called this meeting."

Ivan looks bored and shrugs. "Am I supposed to guess?"

I decide to stop with the games and get to the point. "We know you hired a waiter to drug me during my wedding reception."

"Why would I do that?" Ivan feigns ignorance.

"No idea, why don't you tell me why you would do that?" I shoot back.

"Making such accusations can start a war."

Nico, clearly annoyed by the fucker, moves forward and Ivan's guards put their hands on their weapon holsters ready to pull out their guns. I raise my hand to stop Nico from making another move. Nico instantly stops and steps back but I can tell he is ready to pounce if need be. Carter as well has gone from his relaxed position to a cautious stance.

"I will let this slide once, due to our newly formed alliance but if you try to make another move against me, I will take you out." I step forward and Ivan's two guards again tense up causing me to smirk. "And trust me, even Yuri Petrov wouldn't be able to save you from me."

"I will say this for the last time, I don't know what you're talking about. And next time you make such accusations, I would make sure I have proof." Ivan backs away and his two guards follow suit and leave the warehouse.

"I'm still not satisfied with this." Carter comes to stand next to me. "We may have given him a warning, but what's to stop him again?"

"And we still don't know why he did this," Nico chips in.

Nico is right. Ivan is a smug son of a bitch, but he wouldn't have done something as drugging the Italian Capo without a reason.

"Continue to look into this and in the meantime don't let your guard down when it comes to the Russians."

My phone rings and it's one of my captains who informs me one of my soldiers was found butchered outside one of the family businesses.

He says it's the Irish as they left their signature mark on the now mutilated body. I fill in Nico and Carter and decide it is time to retaliate.

We have allowed the Irish to push their limits for too long, but until now no one was hurt or killed.

Anna

After trying to sleep for three hours, I decided to grab a glass of water to cool my nerves from the kitchen.

Every night I lay awake thinking about when Alessio will come home and if he will be in a bad mood or not and when I do finally fall asleep, I have the same nightmare I always get.

Alessio has not given me a reason to be fearful since the first night but that may just be due to his busy schedule. We barely have interacted for more than a few minutes at a time since our wedding.

I am walking back towards the bedroom when I reach the stairs and hear the elevator chime open. Alessio walks in a few seconds later covered in blood.

I drop the glass of water in my hand at the sight of all the blood. His shirt is completely soaked with some droplets on his neck and face. I am sure his suit jacket and pants are also covered in blood, but the black color makes it hard to tell.

He takes a step towards me, and I step back on instinct. His eyes widen slightly, and he reaches for me but I again step back. I feel a sharp pain going up from the sole of my foot, but I can't take my eyes off the blood. So much blood, just like my nightmares.

Alessio again takes a step forward and as I am about to step back again, he lunges forward at lightning speed and grabs my wrist pulling me forward towards him.

He kneels but doesn't let go of my wrist. I try to pull my wrist free, but he tightens his grip around it further.

The piercing pain from the sole increases and I look down to see Alessio pulling a piece of glass out. I must have stepped on the broken glass from the glass of water I dropped when I stepped back.

"You're going to need stitches." He sighs. "I have a kit upstairs in the bathroom." Alessio gets up and takes a step towards the stairs and stops. He turns around and stares down at me and moves forward. Just as I am about to again take a step back, he grabs my wrist once again. "You really need to stop doing that."

He suddenly picks me up and carries me up to my surprise and heads towards the stairs.

I know I should tell him to put me down but my voice seems to have evaporated. He carries me back to our bedroom bathroom with little effort and gently sits me on the counter.

Alessio grabs a kit from underneath the sink cabinet and puts it on the counter. He takes out gauze and damps it with a disinfecting solution. Alessio grabs my foot and presses the gauze to the wound. It stings slightly but I try and hold steady until he discards the gauze and takes out a medical needle and sutures.

"I don't need stitches," I squeal out in a rush, my voice finally returning. I have had a fear of needles since I was a child. My brothers had to hold me down whenever I had to get shots.

Alessio stares down from his enormous height and frowns. "You clearly need stitches. Your wound is very deep."

As he continues to thread the needle, I slowly try to climb down from the counter in hopes of making an escape.

"Don't," Alessio orders without even turning towards me or taking his eye off the needle. "And stop fidgeting."

"I hate needles and I think a doctor should be doing this," I complain.

"I know what I am doing, I have stitched a number of my own wounds and my brothers' in the past." He takes a step towards me and tries to lift my foot up but I begin to squirm.

Alessio sighs. "Anna, as much as you don't want stitches, I can't have you dying of an infection. I am sure your father wouldn't be too pleased about that."

"I doubt he would care," I unintentionally whisper to myself but notice Alessio stop for a millisecond and looks up before continuing with his task.

The first jab is painful and results in me gripping onto the counter with dear life.

After a few seconds, Alessio gently puts my foot down. "Done," he declares.

I look down at the small but precisely sutured stitches and run a finger over them. "Wow, it looks professionally done."

"You sound surprised." At first, I panic thinking I offended him but then he smirks and looks up at me with his dark brown eyes. "I didn't mean to surprise you by coming home covered in blood. There was a business I had to take care of."

I nod, understanding what type of business he is speaking of.

My papa himself never got his hands dirty as he preferred his men do all the work. He fancied himself giving orders and ruling as though he is king.

My brothers on the other hand were very hands-on, though they tried to keep as much of it away from me as possible. But over the years I would see small signs and clues of what exactly they were involved in.

Alessio takes off his suit jacket and throws it on top of the laundry hamper and begins unbuttoning his shirt. "I need to take a shower."

"I should go to bed," I rasp out and quickly get off the counter and land on my non-stitched foot.

As I'm exiting the bathroom, my eyes land on the mirror and can't help but stare at the now shirtless Alessio.

My eyes wander down his chest to his perfect abs. He begins unbuckling his belt and I feel my face going red and I hurriedly hop out of the bathroom with most of the pressure on one foot before I get caught gawking like a pervert.

I do a quick check of my nightie to see if I have any blood on it from Alessio's clothes or from my cut. Thankfully none transferred over and I settle into bed.

I close my eyes and try to sleep when I hear the bathroom door open and the mattress shift beside me.

"How long are you going to do that?" Alessio murmurs beside me.

I turn around and face Alessio but in the darkness, I can't read his expression but can make out his silhouette. "Do what?" I try to play oblivious but even in darkness, I can make out the frown on Alessio's face.

Alessio reaches over and turns on the side table lamp, producing a warm glow from the light.

Alessio gets up into a sitting position, baring his naked chest. "I know I messed up, but I need you to know I wasn't myself on our wedding night," he trails off, "Someone had put something in my drink at the reception which caused me to believe I was hallucinating when I choked you."

I get up into a sitting position. "You were drugged?" Who would drug Alessio? Of course, several people from the bratva would but not without my papa's permission.

Drugging the Capo of the Italian mafia without the Pakhan's permission is a death sentence.

"I need you to know I would never intentionally hurt you and will never in future."

He waits for me to respond but I'm not sure what to say. He hasn't hurt me since that night and if he was drugged, I can't blame him for it. He didn't purposely intend to hurt me. I also did notice small signs but assumed it was just a headache from a long day.

"I believe you." I give Alessio a reassuring smile. He looks surprised at my statement but returns a small smile.

"Do you have any idea who might have drugged you?" I ask, out of curiosity.

"We suspect Ivan Levin, who works for your father."

I'm thrown off at the mention of Ivan and must have shown it on my face as Alessio narrows his eyes at my reaction. "You look surprised."

"I am, Ivan would never do something like that unless he was ordered by my papa."

Alessio's jaw ticks. "Is that so?"

I realize too late that I may have given too much information which can cause a rift between the bratva and the Italian mafia.

Also despite believing Alessio about being drugged, I don't know I can trust him yet. There are very few people I trust anymore.

"Earlier you had said your father would not care if you died, what did you mean by that?" Alessio interrogates.

"Just that he wouldn't care. My papa only cares about power." I shrink back under his molten eyes piercing into me. Alessio said he wouldn't hurt me, but the fear is still there.

After what feels like an eternity, Alessio sighs and turns off the nightstand lamp. "It's getting late, we can discuss this another time."

I lay back down and try to sleep, but I can't stop wondering why my papa would do this.

This would not benefit him at all and knowing Papa, he doesn't do anything without a reason.

CHAPTER 9

Alessio

L ast night we tortured two Irish soldiers for information on where Ronan Fitzgerald, the current acting boss of the Irish, is hiding.

After Ronan's older brother Shay went to prison, Ronan has been running the family business.

Shay was more rational and gained respect for his honor whereas Ronan is impulsive and erratic.

In the end, the two soldiers were unable to provide any useful information.

Instead, we cut them into pieces and scattered them around Irish owned businesses to send Ronan the message.

When I returned, I hadn't meant to scare Anna and figured she would be asleep at that hour. If I had known I would have changed and showered at the club before returning home.

After explaining to her what happened the night of our wedding, I felt a weight lifted off my shoulders.

I can tell she is still scared of me but at least she knows she has no reason to fear me. I will never give her another reason to fear me again.

What astonished me was when Anna stated Ivan wouldn't have made a move without Yuri's permission. My brothers were just as shocked when I informed them of what Anna had said.

If Yuri was behind it, what reason could he have had and why. He approached me for this alliance, why risk destroying it?

Carter said he would do some digging to try and learn of possible motives for Yuri but at the moment we need to have our guards up. We can't trust Yuri or Bratva if they were behind it.

I get back to the penthouse and find it empty. Greta had messaged me earlier to inform me that she will be leaving early to give her condolences to the family of the soldier who was killed by the Irish.

I hear some music from a distance and follow it. When I arrive in the kitchen, I find classical music playing from the stereo with Anna and Emma in the middle of the kitchen.

Anna is twirling Emma around who then stops and runs into Anna's arms in a giggle fit. Emma tries to catch her breath in-between laughing but has a hard time as another laugh forms.

I have never seen Emma laugh like this.

I try to recall the last time I saw Emma laugh but every birthday party I have thrown her or gift I gave her, she would smile but never like this.

Even when Nico would tease her and play with her, she would smile in excitement but never truly laughed.

I get a strange mix of happiness to see Emma ecstatic but sad that before now she never had this.

"Daddy!" Emma runs towards me and hugs my legs. "Mommy and I made cookies!"

Emma walks towards the counter and tries to reach the plate of cookies, but due to her height she can't reach them. She hops a couple of times and sulks at her failed attempt and turns to Anna.

Anna walks over and grabs the plate of cookies and hands it to Emma. "Here my love, be careful."

Emma grabs the plate with both hands and walks back to me. "Try one Daddy." She looks up from her miniature height with her large brown eyes to mine at me. It pulls on my heartstrings seeing her like this.

"Let me try one." I grab a cookie from the plate and try it. Chocolate chip. It is still warm and chewy. "How did you make these?" I ask Emma.

"My mommy taught me." She grins with such proudness.

Anna grabs the now tilting plate from Emma and places it on the counter. "Let it cool down for a bit."

"Where did you learn to bake?" I ask Anna.

"Yulia, our long-time housemaid, taught me." Anna walks towards the stove and looks inside the oven. "She also taught me how to cook, lunch should be ready in about ten minutes."

"You cooked?"

"I told Greta I would take care of lunch and dinner so she could leave early." She hesitates for a second and pales. "I hope that's okay."

"That's fine."

Anna relaxes and I instantly feel like a jerk for making her fear me again. I don't know how I can make her feel more at ease around me.

Anna begins to take out the dishes and starts to set the table.

Emma grabs my hand and pulls me towards the table. "Come sit, Daddy."

After Anna sets the table and takes out the lasagna from the oven, we sit at the table and have lunch. Emma sits next to Anna and tells me about her day with her mom. Even having lunch excites Emma, as long as she's with Anna that is.

Emma takes a large bite of her lasagna and Anna tucks a piece of Emma's hair behind her ear and smooths her hair down gently.

They seemed to have formed a bond.

Anna looks up from her plate and catches me staring. "Is something wrong? Is the lasagna not good?" She looks at me with unease.

"No, I just have a lot of work I have to take care of. I should get back." I get up from my seat and she grabs my hand quickly, and then lets it go as if it's on fire.

"I also prepared a dish to take for the family of the soldier who was killed. I was going to go later to pay my condolences, I hope that's okay?"

Nico and I had stopped by this morning to pay our respects. Even though he may have only been a soldier, he died for the family, for me.

As Capo, I needed to let the family know that he will never be forgotten and they will be taken care of.

I didn't expect Anna to want to go pay her respects.

Maria never did unless they were high ranking as she stated it was depressing. She and Gia preferred to attend parties and events rather than deal with the depressing side of life. It was probably why they were such good friends, they had similar interests and opinions. They just expressed it in different ways.

"It's fine, just make sure to take Carlo with you."

"I will." Anna gives a small smile.

I send Carlo a quick message informing him of Anna's plans and head back to work.

Anna

I knock on the door of the Russo family home whose son was killed by the Irish.

I don't know much about him but that he was young. He had a wife and two children who are still toddlers.

The door opens to a woman with gray hair tied in a bun, swollen red eyes, and a black dress.

She looks at me and then Carlo who is looming behind me like a shadow and seems confused on who I am. "I don't recall meeting you, were you a friend of my boy Adrian's?"

"I'm Anna Vitale, wife of Alessio Vitale." I stumble out, not yet used to my new surname or that I am now married, despite the large diamond ring on my finger.

The woman's eyes widen. "I'm so sorry, I wasn't aware you were stopping by, please come in." She motions for me to come in. "Oh, let me grab that." She takes a hold of the dish I prepared from my hands.

I follow her into the small house and see several guests speaking in hushed voices amongst themselves. Once they notice me, the room turns into a deadly silence.

I feel out of place and out of my element. I have never visited any of the bratva men's families who were killed or went to their funerals. My papa thought it was beneath him to mingle amongst those of lower ranking.

But growing up my closest friends were the maids and guards. They showed kindness that even my own papa couldn't show me.

I head towards the kitchen wondering if maybe I can help in there, or at least hide from the guests staring at me like I'm some enigma.

The woman who I met at the door is moving dishes most likely from other guests around to make room for mine.

"Let me help." I reach out to move one of the dishes when she stops me.

"No, no, my dear, you shouldn't help with this."

"Please, let me help. I know I can't do much considering your loss but let me help any way I can."

The woman's eyes begin to water, and I startle, thinking I may have said the wrong thing or done something wrong. "Thank you, you don't know how much that means. I know my son didn't have much of an important role, but he was my boy," she quietly weeps.

I hug her. "That's not true, your son's life mattered." I try to soothe her as she cries on my shoulder.

She straightens after a few minutes. "I'm sorry, I didn't mean to cry all over you." She gives me a warm smile. "I realized I didn't even introduce myself, I'm Adele, Adrian's mother. I know his wife Bianca would love to meet you as well."

Adele takes me to meet her daughter-in-law, Bianca.

I was surprised to find out she is only a few years older than me. Her and Adrian were high school sweethearts who married a few years after they graduated.

Unlike the wives of higher-ranking members of the mafia, she wasn't born into this world. Her marriage wasn't political but for love. And now that is over. Her husband, the love of her life, is dead. She is left alone with two children to take care of.

Luckily it seems like she has a supportive mother-in-law and they mentioned Alessio had also stopped by and informed them they and the children will be taken care of.

I was surprised to learn this, but it warmed my heart to know they won't have to struggle financially.

Each day I learn how different Alessio and my papa are. Despite being in the same line of work, they handle things differently.

CHAPTER 10

Alessio

Despite gloomy shadows from mourners at the funeral, it is a warm and bright day. The heat from the sun is scorching into my skin.

I walk down the path of the gravesite to the burial site of the deceased soldier with Anna.

I place my hand on her lower back and guide her through the crowd of stunned individuals.

No one had expected my wife to make an appearance at a soldier's funeral.

I was against Anna coming along at first considering the Irish's continued attacks, but she insisted on going. I also didn't want to deny her the small request when she has finally started getting comfortable around my presence.

I can still see the fear lurking behind her eyes when I appear, but she no longer jumps out of her skin anymore. Which is an improvement.

Once we get to the gravesite, we sit next to Nico and Carter. After the service ends, Anna asks for a moment to speak to Adrian's mom and wife.

As she is talking to his family, I can't help but notice a few men watching Anna with infatuation. After a deadly scowl in their direction, they quickly look away as if they have done nothing wrong.

"If you're going to kill someone, clean-up will be easy considering we're at a gravesite." Nico comes to stand next to me and chuckles.

"I'm surprised Anna came to the funeral." Carter comes to stand on the other side of me. "Did you ask her to come?"

"No, and why is everyone so fascinated with Anna today?" I retort in a bit of anger.

Nico raises his hands in mock surrender. "Just curious considering Maria never used to come. You can also stop giving every man the death stare as well."

"If they would stop staring at Anna like she's a piece of meat, I would," I hiss back. Nico and Carter share a look. "What?"

"Nothing, just didn't think you would care for her. We assumed it would just be a business arrangement between the two of you," Nico says cautiously.

"It is," I say a bit too defensively.

"It's just your relationship with Anna seems different than with Maria's."

"How?"

"For one, you didn't go around giving every guy a look that says you're going to kill them," Nico points out.

I think back to my relationship with Maria. She was beautiful and did get men's attention, but my reaction to Anna is different.

Maria and I were friends before getting married and knew what was expected from each other. Whereas with Anna it started off different and formed into a completely different relationship from what I had with Maria. I can't explain it.

Anna walks back towards me. "Is everything okay?" She stares up at me with those clear blue eyes and I try to figure out what is different between us.

"Let's go home."

Anna

After the funeral, Alessio didn't say much. The drive back was in silence. I could tell he had something on his mind, probably something to do with the Irish.

We get back to the penthouse and as soon as I walk into the family room, Gia storms out.

"You bitch! You're trying to make me look bad!" She comes flying towards me and raises her hand to hit me and I can't help but flinch and close my eyes at the inevitable attack to come.

But after a few seconds, I don't feel anything and open my eyes to see that Alessio is standing in front of me and has grabbed hold of Gia's wrist.

"What the fuck do you think you're doing?" Alessio growls.

"She is trying to ruin my reputation." Gia glares daggers at me while trying to free herself from Alessio's grasp.

"And how exactly is she doing that?"

"I got a call this morning from a friend who told me she went to that dead soldier's family house yesterday and today she went to the funeral."

Alessio rolls his eyes and lets Gia's wrist go causing her to fly back at the sudden release and land on her ass.

She quickly gets up and points her long bright pink fingernail at me. "She's trying to make me look bad and herself look good. Can't you see it?"

"You did that to yourself." Alessio takes a foreboding step towards Gia. "I warned you about disrespecting Anna. Now you will pay the consequences."

Gia crosses her arm and smiles. "Nico won't let you touch me." Her actions seem confident, but her voice shakes with uncertainty.

Alessio smirks. "We both know he won't care." He gives her a terrifying smile that even sends a chill down my spine.

Gia backs away and quickly runs towards the elevator, hitting the button multiple times in the span of a few seconds. Once it arrives, she quickly climbs in and leaves.

I turn to Alessio. "You're not actually going to punish her, are you? She is still your sister-in-law."

"Of course, I am. I warned her and she came here ready to hit you. That can't go without consequences, no matter who she is."

"Won't your brother be upset?"

Alessio laughs. "I doubt he would even care. He hates her guts."

I haven't spent much time with Nico or Gia, so I don't know how their relationship is. I wouldn't be surprised if their marriage was arranged considering Nico's ranking within the mafia. But for

Nico to hate his own wife so much he wouldn't care what happens to her must mean their relationship must be horrible.

Alessio turns to me. "I need to get back to work. There are things I need to handle."

"Does it have to do with the Irish?"

"What do you know about that?" Alessio gives me a questioning look.

"Not much, Greta and Carlo have mentioned it's getting worse."

"It is," Alessio nods in agreement. "In the meantime, it's probably best you and Emma limit your outings and if you do go out, take extra security with you."

"Wait, I'm allowed to go out?" I say in disbelief.

I'm completely thrown off. I didn't think I was allowed out. I was surprised Alessio let me go to Adrian's home or the funeral but assumed it was only because of my duty as a wife of a Capo. To go out casually is not something I thought was possible.

"Why wouldn't you? Did you think I would keep you locked up in the penthouse?"

I don't respond because the truth is I did.

Alessio shakes his head, muttering, "You must truly think I'm a monster," under his breath. "You can go out if you want Anna but take Carlo and the guards with you for safety precautions." Alessio's phone rings and he pulls it out. "I need to go now."

I nod at Alessio who heads to work.

I know things with the Irish are bad but the thought that I can go out makes me happy. For years I have been locked away and assumed it would be the same once I was married. Being given such freedom that was taken away from me brings happiness I didn't know I could have again.

CHAPTER 11

Anna

I t's been weeks since I've seen Alessio. After the funeral, he had gone to work and didn't return home until late. He leaves before I wake up and returns from work after I have gone to sleep.

If it wasn't for his side of the bed being unmade in the morning, I would have thought he wasn't even coming home.

I woke up this morning feeling ill and with some queasiness, which seems to have started a couple of days ago.

I figure it may have to do with something I ate but just in case I made an appointment with the family doctor to get checked out.

My phone vibrates in my coat pocket and I pull it out and see my papa's name flash across the screen.

He has been calling the last several days. I have ignored each and every call. I'm sure Papa is furious but he can't touch me now.

I hit the ignore button and can't help the smile that creeps onto my face.

Since I was a baby, I had to follow each of Papa's rules and could never disobey his orders.

I first learned what it meant to go against Papa when I was six and refused to finish my vegetables.

He threw me out of the house in the middle of winter in the freezing cold in only my nightie.

I had cried and begged Papa to let me back into the house but he had refused. I remember the maids and guards all looking at me with pity but knew it meant death if they tried to help me.

I had balled myself up and had been crying for hours when my brother Nikolai had found me. He knew if he let me in Papa would do something worse as punishment. So, he sat next to me on the ground and pulled me onto his knees and hugged me all night to keep me warm.

He kept saying, "Everything is going to be okay, malyshka," *little one,* over and over again for hours until I fell asleep.

The next morning when Papa finally let me back into the house, he warned me to never go against him or he would do something worse.

For years I did my best to please him and do as he wanted. That is until two years ago I made the mistake of going against him.

I play with the bracelet on my wrist and try not to think of the past but can't help the sting of pain that stabs my heart.

"Let's go to the park, Mama," Emma beams as she hops towards the elevator. I can't help but smile at Emma's excitement and walk towards her as the pain evaporates within seconds.

My bond with Emma has grown to become incredibly strong. Her love and trust in me are unconditional every time I look into her beautiful eyes filled with such innocence.

She may not be my daughter by blood, but she is my daughter in every way that counts. She brings joy and happiness into my life that I never thought I could have again. I will never allow anyone to hurt her or give her a reason to doubt my love for her.

"Hold on, you need to wear your jacket." I grab Emma's jacket from the closet and help her into her jacket. Her brown hair is scattered into a mess.

Every morning I brush out her hair and within an hour it becomes a ball of knots again. I try to smooth out her hair using my hands but when I straighten too quickly, I start to feel nauseous and the room starts to spin.

"Mama?" Emma looks concerned and is frozen on the spot, watching me with wide eyes.

I want to tell her everything is okay and I just need a minute but I don't have time to react before I feel myself falling and everything goes dark.

Alessio

Carter is updating me on the Irish and their movements when my phone vibrates. I look at the name on the screen and it's Carlo, Anna's guard. I pick it up instantly.

"Boss, Anna fainted," Carlo reports. I instantly get up from my chair and Carter follows my lead.

"What happened?" I ask.

"Not sure, she's resting but the doctor is here doing a check-up now."

"I'm on my way." I hang up the call and grab my jacket to leave.

Carter grabs my arm as I'm about to leave. "What happened?"

"Anna fainted and the doctor is there now."

"I'll come with you." Carter grabs his jacket, and I don't miss him checking his weapons in his holster.

I roll my eyes. "We are going to the penthouse, not to war."

Carter just stares at me with indifference. "You should always be prepared for anything."

Carter is always ready for a fight or to kill. It seems to be his way of letting go of pent out frustration and anger.

Carter drives us and it takes longer than usual since Carter drives like a grandma but he's cautious and always checking his surroundings.

I look at my watch and see it's only been 10 minutes since Carlo called.

For the last several weeks I have been avoiding Anna. The day of the funeral I realized she had not only formed a relationship with Emma but had started molding herself into my life.

My marriage to Anna was meant to be for business purposes only and I didn't expect it to be anything more.

We get to the penthouse and once the elevators slide open, I see Carlo standing guard in the family room.

"What happened?" I ask Carlo.

"Not sure, boss. The doctor is still checking Mrs. Vitale out now as we speak."

I turn towards Carter. "I'm going to see if the doctor has an update."

"I'll wait right here." Carter takes a seat on the couch.

I nod to Carter and walk up the stairs when I notice a small ball of dark hair in the hallway.

It is only when I get to the top of the stairs, I realize it is Emma balled up into herself sitting outside our bedroom door.

I stop in front of Emma and kneel down. I gently stroke her hair when she looks up at me with her big round eyes filled with tears.

"What's wrong, mia cara?"

"Mama is sick," Emma sniffles.

"She's going to get better real soon."

"What if she doesn't? What if she goes on vacation again?" Emma whisper sobs.

"She won't."

Emma looks up at me with such innocence. "You promise?"

"I promise," and I mean what I said. I will never break that promise.

The door to our bedroom opens and the family doctor comes out. He is startled at first to see me but recovers quickly.

"Mr. Vitale, I took some blood and will run some tests but nothing to be concerned about. In fact, congratulations are in order, Mrs. Vitale is pregnant."

"Pregnant?" I am shocked at the doctor's assessment but keep my voice even.

"Still early but for now, I recommend she rests and eats in a timely manner. I will also book an appointment with a doctor for the pregnancy."

Anna is pregnant.

Anna

I wake up in my and Alessio's bedroom. I can't remember how I got here or what happened. The last thing I remember is getting ready with Emma to go to the park. *Emma.* I instantly bolt up into a sitting position.

"Careful, you need to rest."

My body instantly jumps at the sudden realization I am not alone. I turn and see Alessio sitting on one of the chairs in the corner.

"What are you doing here?" Usually Alessio's at work around this time.

"Your guard called me and told me you fainted."

I recall heading to the park when I felt ill and things went dark. I must have fainted. Mostly likely due to the fact I skipped breakfast. Anything I eat tends to come out within an hour.

"I've been feeling ill for the last couple of days, it's probably just the flu. Nothing to worry about," I dismiss.

Alessio is silent for a few seconds.

I look around the room. "Where's Emma?"

"Downstairs with Greta."

I start to get out of bed when Alessio rises from the chair. "You need to rest."

"I'm fine, like I said I probably just have flu."

"You're pregnant."

I'm what? I can't be pregnant. "But I can't be, we only... I can't.... How?" I can't form sentences or process what I've just heard.

"The doctor took some blood and is going to run some tests but, in the meantime, you need to rest. He will also book an appointment with an obstetrician."

I still can't process what is happening. I can't be pregnant. I barely know Alessio and we haven't spent much time together. How can we have a child and raise it together?

"I'm going to work from home for the rest of the day. If you need anything, I'll be in my office downstairs."

I don't respond. It's like I lost the ability to form words.

"Anna?"

I turn to Alessio and just nod. He looks at me for a few seconds before he finally leaves the room.

If Papa finds out, he will be ecstatic; he wanted me to have a child right away and told me numerous times leading up to the wedding to have a child as soon as possible. Stating it would buy Alessio's love.

My mother couldn't buy my papa's love by having me; I doubt I could either.

Children are pawns to my papa, to use to gain him power and money. I'm sure once he finds out, he will find a way to use my child to his advantage as well.

I get up from the bed and head downstairs.

Greta is in the living room with Emma doing a puzzle. She looks up at me. "Anna, you should be resting,"

"Mommy, are you okay, I was so worried about you." Emma sniffles from her chair.

I walk over to Emma and kiss the top of her head. "I'm okay, all better now." I turn to Greta. "Where is Alessio?"

"In his office."

I give Emma another kiss on the top of her head. "I'll be right back, my love." And then I head towards Alessio's office.

I knock on his door and hear him say to come in. I walk into his office and close the door behind me.

He looks up from his paperwork and stops what he is doing when he sees me.

I go to stand in the middle of the office. "I need to speak to you about something."

Alessio nods. "Okay, why don't you come take a seat?" He gestures towards the chair in front of his desk.

I hesitate for a second.

Alessio sighs and gets up from his chair and walks towards me. Out of habit, I flinch and take a step back.

He freezes mid-way. "Fuck, you're still scared of me. I thought we were getting past this."

"No," I blurt out quickly. "I just had bad experiences in my papa's office." Alessio gives me a questioning look. "Actually, that's what I wanted to speak to you about. I think it's best we don't tell anyone about me being pregnant yet, including my papa."

Alessio's brows furrow. "Why not?"

I don't want to explain to Alessio my complicated relationship with my papa, if I can even call it that.

"Until we know everything is okay and have all the test results back in, I think it's safer to not tell anyone," I form out an excuse.

Alessio watches me for a minute, I'm sure trying to figure out my lie. "I plan on telling my brothers, but if you wish, we can hold off on telling anyone else including your family until the results come in."

"Thank you." I turn to walk away.

"Anna."

I turn back around to face Alessio. "Is there anything you need to tell me?"

"No," I firmly state.

Alessio nods, and I make my exit.

I know I should tell Alessio about my papa and what kind of person he is. Alessio is my husband and the father of my baby but I don't know if I can trust him yet. Not when I have to take into consideration the safety of my baby now.

To say I have trust issues since my brother Damien's death would be an understatement.

But I can't trust Alessio yet. Not until I am sure he will put the safety of our baby before power, money, or anything else.

CHAPTER 12

Alessio

N ico walks into my office. "We need to talk. We have a problem."

"What kind of problem?"

"Do you remember the guy with all the tattoos we first met at the Petrovs' house before the wedding?"

I recall seeing him for a few seconds. "Dima? What about him?"

"He approached me today and wants to make a deal."

This gets my attention. "What kind of deal?"

"He is willing to give us information on the Petrov family in exchange for money."

"So, he wants to be a rat?" I say in disgust. Rats are the lowest of the low in our business.

"Can we trust him?" I ask Nico.

"I don't know. I hate rats but I don't trust Yuri. We still don't know if he was behind you getting drugged and having an insider in the bratva could be a huge advantage for us."

I lean back in my chair and consider my options. Anna won't like me double crossing her family, but Yuri hasn't kept his end of the deal yet. We agreed to form an alliance, but I've lost my trust in him.

"Let's make a deal with him first and see what kind of information he can provide."

"What if this is a trap by the Russians to test our loyalty?"

"Yuri has failed to keep his end of the deal and if the alliance between the families ends, then it ends."

"And what about Anna?" Nico questions.

"What about Anna? She's my wife and now part of the Vitale family."

Nico nods in acknowledgement.

Anna

My phone rings again and before I even look at my phone, I know it's Papa calling again.

He has left me dozens of voicemails the last several days, but I have ignored each one.

He claims in his messages he wants to know how I'm doing but I know better. He only wants information on Alessio and the Vitale family to gain the upper hand and gain more power.

My papa has never cared about anything else but power.

Once my phone stops ringing, I get a notification saying I have a voicemail.

I'm sure he is furious at my defiance and refusal to answer his calls.

I can't help but get giddy at the thought of Papa not having the upper hand for once.

I toss my phone on top of the bed and walk into the walk-in closet.

I have an appointment with my doctor for an ultrasound today and will even find out the sex of the baby.

At first, I wasn't sure I wanted to know as it made no difference to me, but I needed to get the nursery ready and would like to decorate based on gender.

I decide to keep it simple and wear a long sleeve white t-shirt, jeans and black high heel booties.

I walk out of the walk-in closet and am instantly frozen in place at the appearance of Alessio.

He is sitting on the bed with my phone in his hand.

Since the first night, he has not hurt me. If he was truly drugged, I should have nothing to be afraid of but my body refuses to believe it.

"You have a lot of missed calls from your father." Alessio continues to scroll through my phone. "Is there a reason he is calling you so much or why you are not answering?"

"I don't know why he is calling but I don't want to speak to him. That is why I am ignoring his calls."

Alessio looks at me as if trying to read my face. I can feel my cheeks going red from being under his gaze. "Your father has called me today and wants to have dinner later tonight."

I'm surprised but I guess Papa decided since I won't answer his calls, he would call Alessio instead. I'm already not looking forward to this dinner.

"We should get going, we don't want to be late." Alessio stands up.

"Late?"

"For your doctor's appointment."

"You want to come with me?"

"Why wouldn't I?"

I didn't expect Alessio to want to come or care to take time off work to go with me. "Okay, let's go."

CHAPTER 13

Anna

At the doctors' appointment, we found out the gender of the baby. It's a boy.

I could tell Alessio was excited about the news. I can tell he loves Emma by their interactions and I'm sure he would have been happy either way.

I was just happy to hear everything is good and the baby is healthy.

The delight I felt earlier is now disappearing at having to have dinner with my papa.

We arrive at the restaurant and are greeted by a tall woman with her brown hair styled in a sleek short bob and is wearing a tight black dress and high heels. Her eye makeup is done to give her a cat-eye look and her lips are overdrawn with a bright pink color to give a large pouty lip but only makes them look like balloons.

She smiles at Alessio and sultrily says, "This way Mr. Vitale."

I roll my eyes at her obvious attempt at flirting. She doesn't even look in my direction or acknowledge me. I may as well not even be there.

The woman guides us to our table. Alessio pulls the chair out for me and I take a seat as he takes the seat next to me. The woman bends down so low I'm surprised her cleavage hasn't popped out.

"Is there anything else I can get you?" She is looking at Alessio only.

"No, my wife and I are fine." Alessio doesn't even look in her direction. Which seems to have annoyed her as she leaves in a huff.

"Is this normal?" I ask.

"Is what normal?" Alessio questions.

"Do women just throw themselves at men like that?" It can't be normal, can it? I was homeschooled and was barely allowed to leave the house but I can't imagine women just openly flirting with a married man like this.

Alessio raises an eyebrow in confusion. He couldn't have not noticed, could he? How could he not have when that woman had her chest right up to his face!

He looks back to the woman who greeted us and turns back. "Oh, only the desperate ones," he laughs. He is actually laughing at some woman hitting on him right in front of me. This seems to irritate me for some reason.

"Vitale!" I turn to see my papa and Sergai walking over. "And my beautiful daughter."

Seeing my papa again brings back the memories and pain I want to forget.

Alessio stands and shakes hands with Papa and gives Sergai a nod.

Sergai has that creepy smile that makes me want to crawl out of my skin. "Anna, it's been a long time. How have you been?"

"Fine."

Sergai drops his smile at my answer and looks annoyed. If he expected me to have a conversation with him, he is mistaken.

Papa on the other hand doesn't even notice me and takes a seat across from Alessio and Sergai sits across from me.

A waiter comes and takes our order. I decide to get a simple soup considering everything on the menu makes me sick.

"Anna, you should have something else besides a simple soup, the steak here is delicious," Sergai states while staring at me and having a ghastly smile that makes me want to vomit. Maybe I will vomit on him, that should get him to stop staring at me.

"Anna hasn't been feeling well," Alessio states.

"What's wrong?" Papa looks over towards me.

"Anna and I are expecting," Alessio declares.

I'm taken aback at Alessio announcing my pregnancy. He had let me know earlier he had planned on telling Papa but I had hoped he would wait a bit longer.

Papa smiles. "What great news. Do you know if it's a boy or a girl?"

"A boy."

Papa's smile grows even larger. "That's even better news! Let's celebrate." Papa motions for the waiter and orders a bottle of champagne. I of course can't drink but I doubt Papa would care. To him, I am just an incubator for the baby.

The waiter brings the champagne and a glass of juice for me.

Papa raises his glass. "To the future."

To the future, my baby's future. A future I am already not getting a say in before my baby is even born.

Alessio

After our dinner with Yuri and his right hand Sergai, Anna and I leave the restaurant.

Yuri and Sergai decided to stay and continue drinking, stating he is celebrating. Yuri is overly joyous of the news but Anna on the other hand looked miserable the entire dinner.

I could tell she was not happy having to have dinner with her father. Anna and Yuri have a rocky relationship and from what I have heard of Yuri, it's not a surprise but there seems to be more to it.

The driver holds the door open for Anna and once she is inside the vehicle I go around and enter through the opposite side of the vehicle.

We drive back in silence. Anna stared out the window the entire time. I could tell from her reaction at the restaurant when I told Yuri about Anna being pregnant, she was unhappy. Eventually, the word was going to spread, and not telling Yuri his own daughter is pregnant would be a slap in the face. Which would not help the already strained relationship.

As much as I don't trust Yuri, I can't be openly disrespectful to him until I have proof.

I can't help but wonder what she is hiding from me. She has not been forthcoming about information, but I can't blame her, considering how our marriage started, but eventually we will need to trust each other if we want to build a family.

We get back to the penthouse and Anna excuses herself right away to the bedroom. I'm starting to lose my patience with Anna's closed-off nature. I can't read her mind and she won't tell me anything. I make myself a drink and try to make sense of my wife.

The elevator rings and Nico and Carter stride in.

"I need to change my passcode for the elevator," I murmur under my breath.

"Don't say that. You love us." Nico chuckles as he heads to the table with the alcohol and makes himself a drink. "Got some good news and some bad news again."

"Good news is that Dima is willing to meet us tomorrow." Carter slumps onto the couch.

I take a seat next to Carter. "And what is the bad news?"

"We can't find anything on him." Nico takes a sip of his drink.

"Why are you meeting Dima?" We all turn to the voice coming from near the stairs and see Anna standing there.

"Shit, we didn't know you were there." Nico puts down his drink and starts to head to the elevator. Carter quickly jumps up from the couch and is now joining him.

"I asked, why you are meeting Dima?" Anna repeats.

Nico and Carter turn and stare towards me, unsure of what they should say or do.

I get up and face my wife. "What can you tell us about Dima?"

She crosses her arms and shakes her head. "No, first tell me why you are meeting with Dima."

The room is silent and full of tension. I can see Nico fidgeting back and forth trying to decide if he should run or stay. And then there's Carter who for the first time looks completely and utterly uncomfortable.

I can tell Anna doesn't trust me. We need to start to trust each other and that can't happen without both of us opening up to each other. "Dima wants to provide us with information about the bratva for money."

Anna's brows furrow with confusion. "He would never, he is loyal, unless…" She trails off into a thought.

Nico turns to Anna. "So you're saying he is loyal to Yuri?"

"No, Dima hates my papa, he would never be loyal to him. Dima's loyalties are to my brother Nikolai. If he approached you, it must be my brother's doing."

"Your brother is in prison," Nico points out.

"Nikolai has been in contact with a few selected people even from prison."

"Does that include you?" I inquire.

Anna shakes her head. "My papa has made sure I can't contact any of my brothers." Her tone sounds almost hateful towards Yuri for keeping her away from her brothers.

Nico must have sensed it too. He tilts his head. "Were you close to Nikolai?"

"I was close to all my brothers," she shrugs, "Aren't you all close to one another?"

My relationship with my brothers is unbreakable. We fight for one another and would die for one another. I don't see the Petrov brothers doing that. They seem more the type to step on top of one another to get ahead.

"Why would Nikolai want Dima to provide us with information that could hurt your father?" Carter asks Anna.

Anna nibbles on her lower lip and hesitates before answering, "Nikolai hates my papa. Actually, all my brothers do."

I've suspected Yuri was not the greatest father from the way Anna and him interacted but he is still their father. "Why?"

"Why not?" Anna huffs, "He's a monster who got off on torturing his kids."

A surge of anger boils through me at Yuri laying a hand on Anna. "Does that include you?"

"My brothers protected me most of the time and they had it worse," Anna says with indifference as if being abused is a casual topic.

Anna's confirmation of Yuri's cruelty makes me want to cut Yuri up into pieces. Hell, maybe I will. He has been a useless ally and been nothing but a thorn to my side.

Anna yawns. "If it's okay I think I'm going to head to bed." Her eyes look tired and her body looks frail. Greta had mentioned Anna has not been eating as much as she should considering where she is in her pregnancy but I assumed it was Greta being overly vigilant. Now that I see how delicate Anna looks, I make a note to make sure she eats more. "You should rest."

She nods her head, almost haphazardly, and walks upstairs towards the bedroom.

Nico turns to me. "If Dima is following Nikolai's orders, we should be cautious how we handle this." Being stuck between Yuri and Nikolai Petrov can be very dangerous. If Dima approached us on Nikolai's request, it would be to undermine Yuri's power and overthrow him. Either way, it makes no difference to me. After learning Yuri was abusive to Anna, I could care less what happens to him.

"Let's hear what Dima has to say," I finish my drink in one gulp and slam my glass on the table.

CHAPTER 14

Alessio

Nico and I have been strategizing all morning how to deal with the Irish when Carter walks into my office with Dima following soon after him.

I don't bother with small talk and get to the point. "Why did you approach us?"

Dima shrugs. "I have my reasons."

"Does that reason include Nikolai Petrov?"

"Does it matter?" Dima doesn't acknowledge or refute my question.

"Do you know why Yuri had me drugged?"

"The drink wasn't meant for you. It was meant for Anna." I didn't consider that. "He suspected she wouldn't follow through with the wedding night and needed to make sure Anna became pregnant."

"Why?"

Nico laughs. "Don't tell me, Yuri cares to be a toting grandfather?"

Dima frowns. "No, he wants an heir."

"Anna's child wouldn't be his heir. He would be mine and the future Capo of the Vitale Family," I point out.

Dima shakes his head. "Yuri's plan was always to take Anna's child and raise it."

"What do you mean?" Carter questions.

"Yuri is obsessed with power. He wanted to expand his business into the Vitale territory for years but going to war would be bloody and costly. He doesn't like to get his hands dirty himself. So, he came up with the idea of you and Anna marrying and her giving birth to the next heir. After that, he was going to take the child and raise the Vitale heir. Giving him control of your territory and organization."

Nico shakes his head. "Alessio would never allow it."

"He wouldn't have a choice. Yuri planned on having Alessio killed after Anna gave birth," Dima discloses.

"If Yuri thinks he can kill our brother and take our nephew he is mistaken. We would never let that happen," Nico fumes back in anger.

"Yuri has been planning this for months. He is sure once he has the baby, there won't be much you can do."

"What about Anna? Was she part of this?" I don't want to doubt Anna and I know she wouldn't ever be capable of doing something like this, but I need to be sure.

"No, but if she became a problem, Yuri planned on having Anna killed as well but for now, he plans to give her to Sergai. Sergai has wanted her for a while and after you're dead she will go to him, and Yuri will raise the baby."

Nico makes a disgusted face. "Isn't Sergai 60 or something?"

Dima nods.

"Yuri planned on killing his own daughter?" Carter seems bewildered at what we have learned.

"If Anna or any of his other children stand in his way of getting what he wants, he wouldn't hesitate to take them out."

I start to see red hearing Yuri had planned on not only killing me but Anna and taking our child from the very beginning. On top of that, he was going to give Anna away to Sergai as if she is some toy he can toss to his friend.

If he thinks he can take me out so easily, he's a fool. I will make him regret ever crossing me.

CHAPTER 15

Anna

M ama, look how high I am!" Emma squeals as she rides the swing back and forth. Her dark brunette hair flies around in a mess. I smile at Emma. "I see that. Don't go too high."

After the last several days, I have felt suffocated in the penthouse and needed to get out. My papa has tried to call and like always I ignored his call. Now that he knows I am having a son, I fear what he may want.

The sun has started to set and the playground is almost empty. I get up from the bench I am sitting on and head towards the swings. "Emma, it's time to go home."

"No Mama, I want to play some more," Emma pouts.

"We can come back tomorrow."

"Promise?"

"Promise."

Getting some fresh air was good for both me and Emma. She needs to run and get some exercise. Not to mention mingle with other children.

I grew up locked away my entire life and I don't want that for Emma. She shouldn't be trapped inside her home, or she will feel it is more of a prison than a home. I know something about that.

Emma jumps off the swing and lands on her feet in the sand. She comes running towards me and grabs my hand. "Okay, let's go home."

We start walking through the park with Carlo trailing behind us and almost reach our SUV when I hear a loud shriek coming from a car hitting the brakes quickly. I turn around and see a black windowless van pull up beside us and four men wearing masks and black from head to toe on jump out.

Tony the driver jumps out of the SUV and pulls his gun out of his holster. He aims at one of the men and starts to shoot.

I turn quickly and pick up Emma and start to run. I don't wait for Tony or Carlo.

I hear multiple gunshots going off in the background but all I can think of at this moment is protecting Emma and getting as far away as possible.

I hear loud thumps from heavy boots coming behind me. Then another set of boots can be heard.

I know instantly it is not Tony's as he wears loafers and continue to run as fast as I can. I don't bother looking back and keep running.

Emma tightens her hold around my neck. "Mommy, I'm scared." Her voice is pained and filled with fright but I don't have time to stop and comfort her.

"It's going to be okay," I pant as I continue to run.

The weight of carrying Emma and being 5 months pregnant starts to slow me down. But my instincts tell me to keep running.

I'm about to round a corner when I feel a thin sharp jab on my shoulder. I don't bother to look back and continue to run but after a few seconds, it becomes harder to move my legs. My legs feel like they are being weighed down by cement blocks.

When I know I can't run any further I stop and put Emma down and as I'm about to tell Emma to run, a gloved hand covers my mouth. My brain is telling me to fight but my arms and legs aren't moving and then everything goes dark.

I wake up to Emma's teary face. I instantly get up and run my hands up and down Emma, to check for any injuries.

"Are you okay my love?"

Emma sniffles and hugs me tight and starts to cry.

"It's going to be okay. Daddy will find us," I soothe her.

She continues to shake and cry while pressed into me.

I continue to try and calm Emma and do a quick look around. We are in a small dark cement room with no windows and only a single door that looks like it has a heavy-duty lock on it.

"Mommy, I'm scared." Emma looks up at me with a teary face.

"It's okay, I won't let anything happen to you. Promise."

The door suddenly flings open and three men walk in. I grab Emma and push her behind me with one arm and use my other arm to cover my stomach.

"Mrs. Vitale, you're awake. Let me introduce myself. I am Ronan Fitzgerald."

I instantly recognize his name. He is the acting Irish mafia boss.

"I see from your reaction you know who I am. This is Shane." He nods to the man to the left of him. "And this is Brian." He motions to the man to the right of him. "Your husband butchered his younger brother into pieces only a few days ago."

The man named Brian glares with such anger and hate towards me and Emma.

"My husband's business has nothing to do with me and my daughter. Please let us go." I don't want to beg but for Emma's sake, I will do whatever I need to.

"Doesn't matter if you do or don't. Tell me, Mrs. Vitale, would you like to play a game? I love games. Since I was a child, I would play different games and even came up with some on my own."

I don't know what game he has planned but I want no part in it. When I don't answer, the three men snicker. I can feel Emma shaking behind me.

"Let me tell you the rules of the game. There are five rounds. Each round is more difficult than the last. If you lose one of the rounds, then your daughter has to play in your place."

My eyes widen at the mention of Emma.

"Don't you dare touch my daughter!" I shout. The three men just laugh.

"Then you better not lose," says the second man named Shane.

I know this game isn't a normal game, but I can't risk Emma getting hurt.

"What happens after the fifth round?"

Ronan's eyes gleam in excitement. "If you pass all five rounds, I'll let your daughter live."

I don't miss Ronan's lack of mention of what will happen to me. I will not survive. But as long as Emma lives, I will get through all five rounds no matter what.

"What is the first round?" I ask hesitantly.

The man named Brian steps forward and grabs my arm painfully. I try to claw at him but the second man Shane grabs my other arm.

"Don't fight us or we will take your daughter instead," says Ronan.

Emma starts to cry and I turn my head to Emma. "It's okay, everything is going to be okay. Mommy will be right back." I try to smile at Emma in hopes it will soothe her.

Emma tries to get up and runs towards me, but Ronan pushes her back, causing Emma to fall.

"Don't touch her!" I roar at Ronan but it's no use.

Brian and Shane start to drag me out of the room. I turn to see if Emma is okay, but Ronan has locked the door behind him. I'm relieved that he didn't stay behind. Emma might be alone but she is safer alone then with one of these maniacs.

I am dragged down the hall to another room, similar to the first but twice the size. There is a table and two chairs in the middle of the room and a large carte box in the corner.

I get pushed down onto one of the chairs and my left hand is placed flat on the table. I'm starting to get an uneasy feeling. Ronan sits across the table from me on the other empty chair.

"Remember the rule, you lose or refuse the round, your daughter has to finish the rest of the rounds." I don't miss the excitement in Ronan's voice. I have the urge to claw at his eyes but I can't risk angering them and having them hurt Emma.

Brian goes to the carte placed against the left side of the wall. He starts shuffling around, searching for something. Brian finally finds what he was looking for and returns with a hammer and hands it to Ronan. All my alarms are going off now in my head.

"Last chance, you can give up now." Ronan grins widely.

"I won't let you hurt my daughter."

"She's not even your real daughter," he scoffs.

"She is my daughter," I firmly state.

Ronan grins again and swings the hammer above his head and down on my hand hard. I instantly scream at the horrific pain that passes not only through my hands and fingers but up my arm and throughout my body.

"Do you give up?" he laughs.

"No," I rasp out.

He again swings the hammer but aims at my fingers this time. The ghastly pain from each swing causes me to cry out in pain. Tears fall down my face but I use my other hand to wipe them away. I won't let them have my tears. Men like him live to see the pain and tears of others.

Ronan throws the hammer down at the table in irritation. "Off to round two." Ronan gets up from his chair and starts to remove his belt.

My body reacts on autopilot and I get up from my seat and take a step back.

"Giving up so soon?" Ronan chuckles. "I knew you would eventually back out."

I use my right uninjured hand to hold my pregnant belly in an attempt to shield it. "No, I'm not giving up," I grind out.

Ronan's two men, Brian and Shane come around me and push me down to my knees. Ronan walks around me to my back.

I hear a loud whip sound and a second later my back is hit with sharp pain. I try to hold still but with each whip, my body starts to shake.

After what feels like an hour Ronan drops his belt to the ground with a loud thud. My body sags in relief.

Thankfully I was only whipped on my backside, saving my growing baby inside me.

I look up and see Ronan is angry and is pacing back and forth. All of a sudden he stops and walks towards me. "Round 3."

Before I can react, he punches me in the face. I fall to the ground and Ronan pulls me up by my hair and punches me again and again in the face.

Rather than protect my face I use my arms to protect my belly. After the sixth or seventh punch, I blackout.

When I come to my senses, I'm being dragged back towards the room where I woke up with Emma. I again blackout and wake to hear Emma crying but I can't move.

Every time I try to move, the pain is unbearable. My back feels like it is on fire and my face feels numb. I use whatever energy I can muster up and pull Emma to me.

"It's going to be okay, my love. Everything is going to be okay." I caress her hair and start to sing her favorite lullaby.

"Mama, don't leave me," is the last thing I hear from Emma before everything goes dark again.

CHAPTER 16

Alessio

My mind is racing at what we have learned from Dima. Yuri planned on killing me and taking my unborn child with Anna.

His lack of involvement in dealing with the Irish has been evident but for him to double-cross us was unexpected.

When I agreed on an alliance with the Russians and married Anna, I knew to be wary of them considering their history, but I had expected them to live by their word. In our world, our word is all we have. Break it and we risk future business agreements.

But Yuri only cares about power and gaining it by any means.

"We need to be smart in how we handle Yuri and the Russians," I tell both my brothers Nico and Carter who look as if they are both ready to burn the entire city with the bratva down.

Nico paces back and forth, ready to burst. "We should have never trusted the Russians. Yuri's sons are known to be crazy and irrational, we should have known the father of those psychopaths would be just as worse if not more."

"We can't let Yuri know we are onto him. He may go on the offense and attack before we are prepared."

Carter gets a call and looks at the screen and answers it right away. He looks concerned and looks at me and Nico. "What is it?" I ask.

Carter hesitates. "The Irish attacked Anna and Emma at the park."

"Where are they now?"

Carter doesn't answer me.

"Where the fuck are they?" I shout.

Carter hesitates before answering, "The Irish have them."

The Irish have my pregnant wife and daughter. It is as if history is repeating itself from when Maria was killed.

In a fit of anger, I toss everything on my desk to the wall in frustration. My mind is spinning erratically, and the walls of my office feel like they are closing in on me.

When Maria was killed, I felt a loss of a friend but now it feels as though my world is shattering around me into pieces.

Anna and my child are gone. Taken by the enemy. This can't be happening. I can't lose them.

I feel a hand land on my shoulder. I turn around and hit without thinking. There is a fog blocking my vision. All I can think of is the past and how I am going to lose everything. Another hand lands on my other shoulder and I am pushed up against the wall.

"Alessio, stop, we will find them!" Nico shouts.

My mind clears, and I see it is my brothers in front of me.

"We're going to let you go but you better not hit me again." Carter loosens his grip on me, and Nico follows his lead.

I take a look at my surroundings and see the office is a disaster. It looks

as though a tornado hit. Papers are thrown all across the floor and my laptop is smashed into pieces to the side.

"How could this happen? Where were Anna and Emma's guards!" They were supposed to be protected at all times. I made sure to take extra precautions. I even had extra security hidden in the distance. I hadn't even told Anna, as I didn't want to cause her any panic with the sudden security measures. They were so well concealed that she hadn't even noticed the few times she went out.

Carter rubs the back of his neck. "All the guards are dead, except Carlo. He seems to be missing."

"This had to be an inside job. There is no way the Irish could have taken out all the security guards without someone feeding them information," Nico states.

I turn to Carter. "Find Carlo." With Carlo's disappearance, it's not hard to figure out who the rat is. When I get my hands on him, I am going to make sure he has a slow agonizing death for his actions. I trusted him with my family, and he betrayed me. "We should have everyone within the organization looking for Anna and Emma first."

I walk through the mess I made, grab my jacket from my chair and start to head towards the door.

Nico grabs my arm. "Where are you going?"

"To see Yuri. His daughter is missing and we could use his help in finding Anna and Emma." Despite what I have learned of Yuri, he has connections and the men that could help find them faster. I won't risk Anna and Emma's safety because Yuri is a backstabbing fucker.

Nico nods in agreement. "Let me come with you."

"I will work on getting intel on the Irish and their whereabouts and where they could have taken Anna and Emma in the meantime," Carter proposes.

"Keep me up to date on anything you find," I request over my shoulder as me and Nico walk off the office.

We arrive at the Petrov estate and are stopped at the door.

"The Pakhan is busy," some bushy-haired troll claims.

I want to shoot him in the head and march into Yuri's home. But I need his help, not to make an enemy out of him. Despite knowing his true intentions, I can't let him or the Russians know we have been informed of their plan.

"It's urgent, we wouldn't be here otherwise. Now go be a good little dog you are and get your boss," Nico taunts.

The troll takes a step forward in our direction. Nico's hand twitches in preparation for pulling out his gun. But it would be useless. We are outnumbered by the number of guards on the property. Just as the troll takes another step, the front door swings open.

Dima walks out. "The Pakhan will see them now."

The troll snarls, "Fine." He steps aside allowing me and Nico to go in.

Nico winks back at the troll as we stride by into the Petrov estate.

We follow Dima to the dining room, where Yuri is having dinner with Sergai and Ivan.

My blood boils at seeing them. I want to pull out my gun and kill all three of these fuckers here and now. But Nico and I wouldn't get out of here alive, and we need them at the moment to find my wife and daughter.

Yuri puts down his knife and fork. "I was surprised to hear the Capo of the Vitale family was at my front door at this hour."

I don't bother with the small talk. "Anna and my daughter have been taken by the Irish. We need your help in finding them."

Yuri contemplates for a few seconds. "It seems you wasted your time coming here. I can't get involved with the Irish at this time."

Anger surges through me. "We had a deal. You help us against the Irish and we give you access to our drug trade routes!" I bellow.

"Not to mention the Irish have taken your *daughter,*" Nico snarls in disgust.

Yuri picks up his fork and knife and cuts a piece of his steak. "As I said, I am unable to get involved." He takes a bite of his steak and begins to chew leisurely.

I want to grab the knife and jam it down his throat. How could he care so little for his only daughter? His child. His blood.

"If there is nothing else, I think it's best you leave. Unless you would like to stay for dinner." Yuri motions towards his steak. "It is quite good today."

"No." I try to hold in my rage. I turn without another word and head towards the exit and leave. Nico is right behind me but doesn't say a word until we are back inside our car.

"How could that fucker not even care about his own daughter in the slightest?" Nico shakes his head in disgust. "I'm going to enjoy killing him once this is all over."

"Me too."

We get back to my penthouse and decide to work from the home office considering I destroyed the office at Encore.

As soon as we get to my floor and I exit I see Greta waiting. When she sees me she has a hopeful look on her face. "Any news?"

"No, not yet. We are going to be working from the office here. Carter is on his way. Send him my way as soon as he gets here."

Greta nods as she holds her hands together in prayer. She has raised Emma since Maria's death and I know she has grown very fond of Anna as well.

We get to my office and I open up my laptop to see if I got any emails from the known associates we contacted for help.

Nothing. I slam my fists on the table out of frustration.

"We are going to find them," Nico claims. But his eyes say something else. God knows what Ronan is doing to Anna and Emma right now. If they are even alive. My heart feels like it is being stabbed repeatedly.

Carter walks into the office and shuts the door behind him.

"Any news?" I ask.

Carter doesn't answer but his face says it all. There's nothing.

My phone rings and I take a look at the name and see it's an unknown number. I answer it and put it on speaker for my brothers to hear. "Hello?"

"Alessio! How have you been?" I recognize the voice right away. Ronan Fitzgerald. Nico and Carter's eyes widen in disbelief.

"Where is my wife and daughter?" I roar in fury.

Ronan laughs. "I had heard you got yourself a young hot wife. If I had known how she looked, I would have offered Yuri Petrov a better deal."

My anger is boiling and if I could jump through the phone and strangle Ronan I would.

Carter puts his hand on my arm and shakes his head. Warning me not to take Ronan's bait. I need to get Anna and Emma safe.

"What do you want?" I seethe, trying to hold in my anger to prevent me from saying something that could make things worse.

"What do I want?" Ronan questions. "I want you to fall on your knees. I want to destroy your entire family. I want to take over what remains of the Vitale family once I am done."

Ronan has no plans on returning Anna or Emma. This call was for him to gloat. "If you lay one hand on my wife and daughter," I warn.

"Or what?" Ronan interjects. "I can do whatever I want. In fact, I am considering playing a game my father used to play with me and my brother when we were younger."

I know what game Ronan is talking about. My father used to tell us how the former Fitzgerald boss used to make his sons go through rounds of torture. Each round is worse than the previous. If one of them failed or refused, the other brother would have to take his place. It was fucked up. I won't let Anna and Emma go through that.

"Name your price, if you want me, I will trade myself for Anna and Emma."

Nico and Carter share a look. They are against this, but I will do whatever it takes to get my family back. Even if it means sacrificing myself.

"Nope, I'm not done playing with my new toys yet." Ronan hangs up the call.

I try to call back but it goes straight to voicemail. He must have turned his phone off. I throw my phone against the wall causing it to crack before hitting the ground.

Carter's phone rings. "I'll be right back." He walks out of the office.

I slump down into my chair as the facts sink in. Ronan has my wife and daughter and is probably torturing them as we speak.

I look up at my brother Nico and for once he is silent.

CHAPTER 17

Anna

D amien." I crawl to my brother who lays motionless on the ground. He is covered in blood. I can't tell where all the blood is coming from. As I get closer, my jeans get soaked in his blood. I feel for a pulse but don't feel anything. He is still warm. "Damien!" I cry. But he doesn't respond. I try to shake him but nothing.

"I warned you, Anna." I look up towards the harsh voice and I'm yanked up by my hair. I scream in agony but not for the physical pain but the emotional pain from seeing my amazing older brother.

Alessio

Carter barges into the office in a hurry. "I think I got something." He comes around my desk and grabs the laptop.

"What?" I ask in disbelief.

Carter begins to type on the laptop. "That was Dima on the phone, he asked to meet me outside. He said Anna has a bracelet with a tracking chip and gave me the username and passcode to track her."

"Why didn't Yuri tell us this earlier when we went over to his place for help?" Nico questions.

"Dima said he doesn't know." Carter finishes typing and we get a location. It's outside the city limits near the docks.

"Wait, if Yuri doesn't know, how does Dima? How do we know this isn't a trap? We just met the guy today and we haven't even verified what he told us previously to be the truth. For all we know he is playing us," Nico inquiries.

Nico is right. "We don't know if this isn't a trap. But I'm willing to take the risk."

"Okay, in that case we're with you," Nico declares.

I write down the location coordinates and we head out.

We get to the abandoned warehouse where the coordinates for Anna's tracking chip is. We are parked just outside the gates.

Carter surveys the surroundings. "I'm going to the roof of the other building. I'll take out anyone that comes near you from up there."

Carter takes out his sniper and sprints towards one of the buildings. He always had a good shot but is an even better marksman. He could take anyone out from any distance.

Nico double checks his ammunition. "I called in our most loyal soldiers only. They will hit the warehouse from the north while we move in from the south."

"Make sure they know to leave Ronan alive. I'm not done with him," I growl.

Nico takes out his phone and sends out a quick text. "Done."

"Okay, let's move in."

ANNA

I hear shots. I can't tell where they are coming from.

"Mama," Emma cries. I feel her pressing into my side, but I can't move. No matter how hard I try I can't move. I force my eyes to peel open. They feel sticky and my lashes stick together like glue. When I finally open my eyes, my vision is blurry and certain areas have splotches of red.

"Emma," I try to call out but my voice comes out hoarse and painful.

Emma pushes herself further into me and a piercing pain goes up my body. I hiss at the pain but try to hold it in. I don't want to scare Emma. She wraps her little arms around me and I feel her warm lips as she gives me a kiss on the cheek.

The shots are getting louder and I hear screams. I still can't tell which direction they are coming from.

Then there is silence. A deadly eerie silence.

Alessio

We have killed most of Ronan's men and those that weren't killed were left alive to get intel.

Ronan himself is nowhere to be seen. I get to the end of a hallway and notice a door with a lock. I run towards the door and break the lock by hitting it with the back of my gun.

Once I enter, I am shaken at what I see.

"Daddy!" Emma runs towards me and I grab her into my arms. I pull her towards me and give her a kiss. I look over her small body and see she doesn't have a single scratch on her. She is okay.

Nico comes in from behind me. "Shit!"

I hand him Emma. "Go with your uncle." He takes her into his arms instantly.

I walk further into the room. Anna is lying motionlessly on the ground. She is bloodied and bruised. I can barely recognize her if it was not for her golden hair.

I kneel down and pull her into my arms as I pick her up. She makes a mangled noise at being moved that stabs me in the heart. I kiss the top of her head. "It's going to be okay." And I carry her out.

CHAPTER 18

Alessio

We get to the hospital at the speed of light, breaking every speed limit on our way and I carry Anna into the emergency room. The wide-eyed nurse quickly calls for a doctor and guides us to an empty bed.

I was told to wait outside as the doctor checks out Anna, but I refused. I can tell from the staffs' hatred-filled looks they either knew who I am or suspect I did this to my wife or possibly both.

Regardless it didn't matter, I wasn't going to leave Anna alone. After several tests, Anna is finally moved to a private room.

Nico and Carter walk into the room.

"Where is Emma?" I ask.

"Back at the penthouse with Greta," Nico informs. "How is she?"

The doctor walks in at that moment and halts once he sees us. "I-I can come back later. I wasn't aware there were guests," he stammers. Clearly, he too has heard of our reputation.

"It's okay, whatever you have to say, you can say in front of my brothers," I advise the doctor.

The doctor begins fidgeting with his folder and then drops the folder to the ground scattering all the paperwork.

"For fucks sake," Nico swears.

"I'm… I'm sorry," the doctor apologizes.

I give Nico a warning look. I've already called the family doctor, Dr. Watson, but in the meantime, we don't need the doctors at the hospital who are treating Anna shitting themselves.

The doctor gathers up the paperwork and tries again. "Mr. Vitale, your wife suffered a number of injuries. Her right hand and fingers are broken. Which is why we have placed a cast. She has multiple cuts and slashes on her back and thighs. Her face is quite bruised up but nothing that will require surgery. Her injuries should eventually heal with time."

"And the baby?" I probe.

"We did an ultrasound and the baby surprisingly looks to be okay. I do recommend Mrs. Vitale rests and to make an appointment with an obstetrician right away."

"How soon can she be discharged?"

The doctor is surprised by my question but quickly looks down. "I don't recommend it."

"How soon?" I repeat.

The nervous doctor sighs. "Now technically." The doctor quickly writes something on a pad. "Here's a prescription to help heal the cuts on her back." He hands the prescription to me with shaking hands. "I will get the paperwork ready." The doctor speed walks out of the room.

Nico shakes his head at the doctor's quick exit and turns to me. "Is it a good idea to move Anna so quickly?"

"We don't have a choice. Ronan is still out there. The safest place for her is back home."

CHAPTER 19

Alessio

Anna is back home and has been checked by Dr. Watson upon arrival. There seem to be no life-threatening injuries but every time I look at Anna, I am filled with rage and the need to torture Ronan for what he did to her.

Since bringing her home last night she has not woken up. Dr. Watson stated it was normal as she needed to rest after the ordeal she has gone through. But every minute that goes by and she doesn't wake up worries me.

I am heading towards the bedroom when I notice the door is slightly ajar.

Once I enter the room, I see Emma is on the bed kneeling over Anna. She is still in her pajamas and her dark brown hair is scattered in a mess.

After Anna was checked out, Dr. Watson looked over Emma and advised she is perfectly fine. Not a single injury.

"Mia Cara, what are you doing here?"

Emma turns around and puts her index finger to her mouth. "Shhhh, Mommy's asleep," she whispers.

I smile and kneel down beside the bed to her eye level. "You shouldn't be in here," I whisper back.

Emma shouldn't have to see Anna like this. I don't know the damage of being kidnapped and what they went through has done to my daughter.

Nico suggested Emma should go through counseling but in our line of business going to a therapist is frowned upon and can be used against us. But for Emma's sake, I will do whatever it takes to heal her.

"How would you like to see a special doctor?" I ask.

Emma pouts. "Why?"

"For what you and Mommy went through. If you're hurt anywhere or want to talk to anyone, they can help."

Emma shakes her head. "I'm not hurt. Mommy protected me. I don't need to see a doctor. I just need Mommy."

"She did?"

"She did," Emma states in pride.

I give my daughter a kiss on the top of her head. At one point I didn't think I would ever be able to hold my daughter again.

"You really love your mommy, huh?"

"I do!" Emma whisper yells.

"Even more than me?" I tease.

Emma pauses for a second and smiles. "I love you, Daddy, but Mommy's my favorite."

Maybe at any other time, those words would have hurt me but instead hearing how much Emma loves Anna warms my heart.

Anna sacrificed herself to protect Emma. She has been raising Emma as if she was her own. I was always worried about what losing Maria and not having a mother would do to Emma. I am pleased to see that Emma has a mother that loves and cares for her.

I pull Emma towards me and pick her up and give her a dozen kisses on her face causing her to squeal in laughter. "Let's go downstairs and let Mommy rest."

Anna

I wake up in ghastly pain. My vision is still a bit blurry but better from last time.

I look around my surroundings and see that I am back at the penthouse. I can't seem to figure out how I got here. I try to move my arm to feel for Emma but my arm is immobile and heavy. I shift too quickly causing me to yelp from the sharp pain.

The door flings open a few seconds later, and Greta runs inside. "Anna, don't move. You will only hurt yourself. Let me get Mr. Vitale, he has been waiting for you to wake up." She runs out of the room in a frenzy.

Despite Greta's warning, I try and pull myself into a sitting position which causes the sharp pain to increase.

After a second failed attempt to get up, I decide to crumble back down on to the bed. I stare at the ceiling trying to figure out what is happening.

Every time I move the slightest, the pain takes me back to the room with Ronan and his men. They laughed with each bit of pain they inflicted on me.

Alessio walks into the room and stares at me in disbelief. "You're awake." He walks around the bed to my side and hovers over me. "Greta is calling Dr. Watson. He will be here soon to take a look at you."

"Where's Emma?" I rasp my throat feeling dry.

Alessio smiles. "She's fine, she is downstairs with Greta. You protected her."

A tear I've been holding in since waking up falls down my face. Not sure out of relief or pain.

Alessio sits down on the bed next to me and using the back of his finger wipes away the tears. "You're in pain. You can't have strong medication because of the baby but I'll ask Dr. Watson if there is something else you can have."

"The baby," I croak. I forgot about the baby.

"He's fine. An ultrasound was done at the hospital last night and I've made an appointment with the obstetrician in a couple of days who will come here with all her equipment to check you out fully."

I don't remember going to the hospital or how I got here. But I don't have the energy to ask. All I needed to know is Emma and the baby is okay.

Alessio

Anna had woken up briefly to ask about Emma and the baby but had fallen back asleep.

Once Dr. Watson finally arrived, he verified that it was normal. Anna will need a lot of rest to heal.

After making sure Emma had everything she needed, I headed to the club, Encore.

Once I arrive, I head straight downstairs to the underground basement where we have been keeping the Irish who survived the attack.

Nico is already waiting for me in the hallway.

"What do you have?" I ask.

"None of them know where Ronan is."

"Then why did you call me down here?" I bark in frustration.

Nico slowly smiles. "One of the men we captured, his name is Brian and he helped Ronan torture Anna."

I snap my head towards Nico. "Where is he?"

"With Carter," Nico grins.

Knowing Carter, he probably did a number on him. Nico points towards one of the rooms. I head straight there.

My rage is blistering and I need something or someone to take my aggression out on.

I walk into the room and find a man tied to a chair with no shirt or pants. He is completely bloodied and bruised.

I walk straight towards him and he looks up at me but before he can say anything or react, I kick him hard, resulting in him and the chair he's tied to falling backward with a loud thump.

I step on his neck. "You helped Ronan torture my wife!" I roar.

He slithers under my foot from the lack of oxygen. When his eyes are about to pop out of his sockets, I release him. I'm not going to let him die this easily.

The Irish takes heaving breaths as he sucks in air. "You killed my brother," he coughs in heavy breaths.

Carter comes to stand next to me. "His brother was one of the men who we killed to send Ronan a message a few weeks back."

"My only regret is not finishing off your whore of a wife," Brian spits.

I take off my jacket and toss it to the side and roll up my sleeves. I crouch down and give him a cold smile. "You're going to regret ever laying a hand on my wife."

CHAPTER 20

Anna

I woke up from the same nightmare I've had for the last two years. Only this time I didn't wake up from the nightmare. I wake up to the memories of Ronan.

I look around and see it's dark. I'm not sure what time it is but I can see the moonlight coming through the curtains. I look to my side and see Alessio is asleep next to me.

It must be late considering Alessio is here. Usually, he doesn't come home from work until well after I have gone to sleep.

Every time I close my eyes, I go back to my nightmare. When I open my eyes, I am reminded of Ronan.

The pain is unbearable. I can't close my eyes, but I can't keep them open either.

I force myself to get up. The alarming agony I feel throughout my body is nothing compared to the pain I feel in my heart.

Once I am up in a sitting position, I slide out of bed and make my way towards the door.

It takes longer than expected since I can only take small steps.

Once I'm in the hall I feel an emptiness. I continue to walk down the hall and down the stairs, ignoring the pain vibrating through my body.

I get to the family room but despite the uncanny silence, I can't stop the memories from filling my mind. I feel as though I am being suffocated by the past and the present.

I start to have a hard time breathing and look around the room for help. I notice the balcony door and limp towards it, needing to get out of the stuffed room.

I push open the door and walk outside to the balcony.

The cold October air hits my face, causing me to shudder at the coldness. Yet the fresh air does nothing to ease the pain in my soul.

I want the pain to stop. I want the memories to go away. I try to focus on anything else but the pain. But it won't leave me. It has etched itself into the deepest parts of my soul and refuses to let go.

I hear cars honking from a distance and try to focus on that. I continue to focus on the noise from the traffic below.

Without even realizing I've made my way to the end and I'm standing on top of a chair at the edge of the balcony.

I look down and see the warm yellow glow from streetlamps.

I start to feel at ease at seeing the warm glow. All I can now feel is the wind through my hair. My mind is clear as I focus below.

I can't help but wonder if this is what my mother felt before she jumped. Did she have a similar pain? Did jumping make the pain go away?

I take a step forward towards the edge and close my eyes. Ready for the pain to stop.

Alessio

I feel to the side and my arm feels nothing but coldness. I get up immediately from the odd sensation.

I look to my left and see Anna's side of the bed is empty. I grab my gun from the dresser in case there is an intruder and head towards the exit.

With Carlo still missing and Ronan still out there, I can't take the risk.

I walk down the hallway and stop in front of Emma's room. I peek in and see her soundly asleep on her bed.

I make my way downstairs and feel a cold breeze towards the balcony and see Anna through the windows. She is standing on top of a chair at the edge of the balcony.

I throw the gun onto the couch and run towards her as fast as I can. She takes a step forward and I jump forward and grab onto her hand and pull her back.

She falls back into me, and I catch her in my arms.

I take her inside and put her down on the couch. She looks up at me in confusion.

My heart feels like it's about to explode. I slump down onto the couch next to Anna and lay back and release a sigh of relief.

That was close. One second later and Anna would have been gone.

I turn towards Anna to get answers. "What were you doing?"

She doesn't answer.

"You could have died!"

Again silence.

I get up, my anger now steaming. "Anna, answer me!" I shout.

She just sits there silently staring at me. I start to pace back and forth to try and make sense of this situation.

After a few minutes, I finally calm down. I look at Anna. My wife. Battered and bruised.

I kneel in front of her and grab her hands into mine. Her one hand is bandaged completely from being broken.

"Don't *ever* do that again."

She doesn't respond. Just watches me with her beautiful blue eyes.

I pick her back up in my arms and head back upstairs. Once back in our bedroom, I lightly lay her back into bed.

I lay on my side and look at the clock. It's almost 4 am and I need to be back at work in a few hours.

The last several days, I've barely slept with everything that's happened. I am physically exhausted, but I can't let myself fall asleep.

I turn towards Anna and see she is wide awake. I can't help but wonder if once I fall asleep, she might try something again.

I wrap my arms around her and pull her into me. She wiggles in my hold. "Anna, please just go to sleep." She wiggles again but I don't let go.

After she finally stops moving around, I only then let myself fall asleep.

I feel a weird sensation on my side, almost like a kick. It's light but annoying.

I open my eyes and see it's daylight. I have Anna still wrapped and pressed into me.

I feel the hit again. I look down towards the hit and realize it's the baby. The baby is kicking inside Anna's belly.

I put my hand on Anna's small bump and feel the baby kick again. I smile at the bump, my son. I almost lost him last night.

Anna is still asleep.

"Let your mom sleep," I whisper to the baby bump.

I slide my arm from underneath Anna and pull away. She shifts in her sleep and turns around.

Her back now faces me and with it the dark ghastly slashes on her back visible from her silk nightie.

I can't even fathom the pain she went through and is still going through.

I lightly kiss her shoulder blade and sneak out of bed without disturbing Anna. I grab my clothes, shower and change, and head downstairs.

Nico is in the living room with Emma on his lap. Nico tickles Emma who giggles back.

"Daddy!" Emma crawls out of Nico's lap and stands on the couch. "Is Mommy awake yet?"

"No, she's still sleeping." I give her a kiss on the cheek.

Emma frowns. "For how long?"

"She needs to rest, Mia Cara. Why don't you get Greta to make you something for breakfast?"

Emma hops off the couch with an, "okay," and waddles towards the kitchen.

Nico stands. "Is everything okay?"

I check to see Emma is not within hearing distance. "No, Anna tried to jump off the balcony last night."

"She what?"

"I woke up to her missing. Thankfully I made it in time before she could jump. But I think for the time being I should work from home. I need to keep an eye on Anna."

Nico nods. "Let me know if you need anything else."

"I need you to find Ronan and bring him to me."

"I will, no matter what it takes."

CHAPTER 21

Anna

D amien?" "I warned you, Anna!" my papa barks. He pulls me to my feet by my hair.

"Please Papa, save Damien," I cry.

"He made his choice and betrayed me," he sneers. "Will you follow him?"

I look at my amazing older brother Damien. He is covered in blood. Lifeless.

I try to go towards him but Papa's grip on my hair is too tight. I can feel my hair being pulled from my scalp but I don't care. I need to go to my brother. Papa lets me go and I fall to the ground on my knees. I hear a click and turn around and see my papa holding a gun to my head. "What is your choice going to be, Anna?"

I open my eyes and see Emma hovering over me.

"Mommy, you're awake!" she squeaks. She lightly places her small hand on my cheek. "I was worried."

I want to tell her it's okay. I'm okay. But it's not okay. I'm not okay.

Alessio walks into the room. "Emma! I told you not to disturb your mom." He grabs Emma by the waist and places her on the ground. "Go play in your room. Your mom needs rest."

Emma pouts. "But I want to be with Mommy."

Alessio crosses his arms. "Emma," he warns.

"Fine." She stomps out of the room and a few seconds later a door slams shut.

Alessio shakes his head and turns towards me. "Anna, how are you feeling?"

I don't want to think about how I'm feeling. It's easier that way. I turn away from Alessio and stare at the wall. Alessio doesn't get the hint since he comes around the bed and blocks my view.

He kneels to my eye level. "Greta made you some soup." He points towards the nightstand. "You haven't eaten in a while. Dr. Watson has been giving you nutrients from an IV, but you should start eating. Do you need help?"

I want to ignore him but I get the feeling he won't leave until I answer. And I definitely don't need his help. "No," I rasp out.

He looks at me for a few seconds. Not sure what he is trying to see. Eventually, he sighs. "I'll check back on you later." He gets up and leaves.

Once I hear the door shut, I go back to my own mental hell.

Alessio

I'm working in the home office with Nico when Greta knocks on the door. She peeps in. "I'm sorry to disturb you Mr. Vitale but Yuri Petrov is here."

What could he want? He couldn't care to help us find his own daughter and now he is here. I'm sure he has an alternative motive.

I stand from my chair and exit the office with Nico following behind.

We get to the living room and find Yuri and Sergai waiting. I want to knock his smug face out.

"What the hell do you want?" I ask Yuri with little patience.

"I came to see my daughter and to see how my grandson is doing."

"*My wife* and *son* are doing just fine. You can leave now."

Yuri doesn't move. "I've been thinking, I don't think my daughter is safe here. I think it's best that she stays at home with me for the time being."

"Anna is not going anywhere," I growl. "She is my wife, and she is staying here. Now you can either leave on your own two feet or I will have my guards throw you out."

Yuri glares at me. "Don't forget who I am."

"Don't forget who *I am*. Now get the fuck out!" I roar.

Yuri and Sergai don't move, and Nico pulls out his phone to call the guards.

Yuri raises his hand. "We will leave but this is not over."

Yuri and Sergai finally leave but not before Sergai gives a passing glare. I'm going to enjoy cutting him up after I'm done with his boss.

"We have to take care of Yuri. He is a threat," Nico points out.

"I know, but we can't be fighting the Irish and Russians at the same time. Yuri won't make a move until Anna has the baby. In the meantime, our focus should be finding Ronan."

Nico nods in agreement.

Anna

I didn't want to move or eat but the hunger was too strong. I finally caved and had the soup Greta made.

I spend most of my time lying in bed and trying to do anything but think of the past. It's a difficult challenge. No matter how hard I try, I go back to the memories I want to forget.

In the past after Damien died, I had my brothers around me to protect me. To tell me everything is going to be okay but now I have no one. Only pain remains.

Greta comes in to check on me multiple times a day and drops off a tray of food each time. Half the time I don't have the energy to get up and eat. But after she insisted she feed me, I decided to eat a bit to pacify her.

It's been weeks since I have returned to the penthouse, but I feel I am still imprisoned.

Dr. Watson stopped by and advised me that my injuries are healing well. But he can't see the injuries deep in my soul. Those aren't healing no matter how much time goes by.

Instead, they continue to bleed out and kill me from the inside.

A doctor who is a specialist in dealing with pregnancies also stopped by a couple of times to check on the baby. I didn't really care to chat or make nice talk. She did her exam and advised everything was good with the baby.

Emma usually sneaks in and tells me about her day and I try to smile but it gets harder and harder each day.

I haven't seen Emma in a couple of days. I assume Alessio is keeping her away. Probably for the best considering what a mess I am.

I can tell Alessio is concerned and is constantly either having Greta check up on me or he does himself.

At night if I move the slightest or get up to go to the washroom, he wakes up alert.

He must think I am going to jump again but the truth is I don't even remember how I got to the edge of the balcony. One minute I was trying to breathe and the next I was at the edge.

I'm not suicidal. I don't want to die. I just wanted the pain and the memories to go away.

The sun is setting and the orange-yellow glow from the sun comes through the curtains. I walk over to the window and sit on the windowsill.

Aside from my hand, most of the injuries have healed and the bruises have faded.

Down below on the street, I see people walking towards their destinations.

I can't help but wonder where they are going. I decide to come up with a story for each person that walks by.

A man on his phone, I decide, is late due to a business meeting and is rushing to make it home on time to his loving wife and children. A woman with shopping bags is heading home to her family with gifts she bought. A group of girls are dressed and ready to go out for drinks before partying.

Then I see a man with blonde hair. He resembles my brother Maxim. It's hard to tell from how high up I am.

It's the way he leans so casually against the building wall on the opposite side of the street that reminds me so much of Maxim.

I haven't seen Maxim in almost two years. He left soon after Damien died. A few months later Alek was sent to a mental institution and then Nikolai to prison. They were my only lifeline and then they were gone.

The bedroom door opens and Alessio walks in. He looks around the room in fear until he sees me near the window and pauses. "What are you doing there?" His expression is mixed with concern and wary.

I shrug. "I got tired of laying in bed all day."

"Dr. Watson said it would be good for you to go out or move around. Maybe you can join us for dinner tonight?"

"Maybe."

Alessio is silent for a second. "Emma misses you."

I miss Emma as well but I can't force myself to pretend and put up an act anymore.

I turn away from Alessio and go back towards the window and continue gazing out. The blonde man from earlier is gone.

Left behind is the pain of loss.

CHAPTER 22

Alessio

Anna is physically healing well but mentally I'm concerned. She hasn't tried anything drastic since that night on the balcony.

Just in case, I have Greta watching her to make sure she is never left alone for long periods.

Despite wanting to be near, I had to stop working from home the last couple of days after several problems needed my immediate attention.

The hospital reported Anna's injuries to the police who have insisted on speaking to her and checking on her welfare. The family lawyer has blocked their attempts for now but eventually, Anna will have to make a statement.

The Irish continue to cause havoc and Ronan is still nowhere to be found.

There have been rumors of Ronan approaching the Chicago-based Italian Mancini crime family for an alliance.

The Mancinis are a powerful family and control the entire mid-western region. They could cause trouble for us if they side with Ronan.

Yuri and the Bratva have also gone silent. I have Carter and some loyal soldiers keeping an eye on Yuri for now, but eventually, I will have to make a move to protect my family.

Despite Anna saying she might join us for dinner she never did. She instead spent hours looking out the window. I wasn't sure if she was searching for someone or something.

It's past midnight when I return to the penthouse. Greta is asleep in a sitting position on the couch. I lightly shake her awake. Greta gets up instantly and stands up. "I'm sorry Mr. Vitale, I didn't mean to fall asleep," she mumbles in a daze.

"It's okay, Greta. Go home and sleep."

Greta nods and grabs her jacket and purse before heading out. You can see she is exhausted and tired from the long hours.

I send a quick text to my accountant to have Greta's salary raised. She deserves it after everything.

Once I get upstairs, I go to Emma's room. She is sleeping in her bed with her dark hair ruffled in a mess all over her face. I push it off her face and give her a kiss on the cheek.

Once I get to my bedroom, I hear an inaudible distorted noise in the dark. I get closer to the bed and realize it's Anna. She seems to be having a nightmare and is crying in her sleep.

She had nightmares before she was kidnapped and I suspected it was due to her fear of me. For all I know, she could still be having those same nightmares or they could be from her time being kidnapped.

Regardless I am to be blamed for her nightmares and suffering.

I get out of my clothes and get into bed in only my boxer briefs. I pull Anna towards me and wrap my arms around her.

She moves around a few times but then stops. Her breathing evens out and her tears stop.

Anna

I had another nightmare last night but unlike how it always ends with my brother's death it was different this time. Instead, I dreamt of the good times I had with my brother Damien.

I was surprised to find myself pressed into Alessio's side when I woke up but I didn't care. I woke up in a good mood for the first time in weeks.

I try to get out of bed but Alessio's arms are like bands of steel. Every time I try to get up, he tightens his hold around me.

Eventually, I gave up and decide to go back to sleep. His body is warm and surprisingly comfortable.

The next time I wake up Alessio is gone. But the happy memories from the dreams are still there.

I get up and decide to shower and get dressed.

The majority of my clothes don't fit me anymore, so I have to wear a very snug fit dark purple dress and black flats.

I head downstairs towards the kitchen and find Greta cooking.

To say she is shocked to see me would be an understatement. "Anna, what are you doing? You should be resting."

Emma, who is eating pancakes at the table, drops her fork and runs towards me. "Mommy, you're back!" She wraps her arms around my legs.

I forgot how much she melted my heart. I kneel down to her level which is harder than I expected with my baby bump and tight dress. I give her a tight hug and kiss her twice on the cheek. "I've missed you, my love."

"I've missed you too, Mommy!" Emma's hold around me squeezes. I can't help but laugh.

I try to get up but end up requiring some assistance from Greta since my bump made it hard for me to get up.

Greta guides me to the table. "Anna, come sit. I will get some breakfast ready for you."

Emma pulls out the chair next to her. "Mommy, come sit next to me."

I take the seat and Greta fills up a plate with an assortment of fruits, muffins, eggs, and pancakes. It is more than I can possibly eat but decide to try each one.

"My love, how would you like to go online shopping with me later?" I ask Emma in between bites. I need new clothes and online shopping seems the best and safest option right now.

Emma smiles with syrup dripping from her mouth. "Let's go shopping!" she squeals.

Alessio

I get a text from Greta, advising me that Anna came down for breakfast today.

I couldn't believe what I was reading. I was over the moon to hear Anna made some progress.

She has been through so much and it has taken a toll on her mentally. At one point I feared she may never come out of it.

I send a quick text to the guards to keep an eye out in case she decides to wander out. I have doubled the guards around Anna and Emma since the kidnapping.

"What are you smiling about?" Nico questions.

"Anna left her room today," I say with a smile.

Nico looks surprised. "That's great! I was starting to get concerned." Nico pauses for a second. "Since Anna is doing better maybe it's a good time to have a conversation."

I narrow my eyes at Nico. "About what?"

"There have been several rumors going around. That Anna is broken or mentally unstable. Some of your underbosses and captains feel she is not a good fit to be the Capo's wife."

"Who the fuck said this!" I growl. "I will shoot them in the head for daring to say such bullshit!"

"Look, it's just a rumor. We need to put them to rest. The Bianchis are having a Thanksgiving dinner party next week. Bringing Anna and making an appearance will finally put those rumors to rest. Not to mention since the wedding, you haven't brought Anna to any party or family event. People tend to talk."

Thomas Bianchi is one of my underbosses and is having a dinner party for Thanksgiving. All the other underbosses and captains and their families will be there.

I consider it for a moment. It's not safe considering Ronan has not been caught yet. But I can't keep Anna locked up forever.

She is also my wife and the mother of my unborn son. Everyone needs to know she is not unstable or going anywhere, and her place is beside me. Forever.

"Fine, but we need to take extra measures for security."

Nico grins. "I will personally make sure it's taken care of."

Anna

After spending several hours shopping online, I spent some time with Emma doing a puzzle. Eventually, I get exhausted and lay on the couch to rest.

Emma comes to sit next to me and puts her ear onto my stomach.

She scrunches up her nose. "Greta said there's a baby in there. I don't hear it."

I smile at Emma's attempt to hear the baby. When the baby kicks, she straightens up in shock. "He kicked me!" I burst out laughing at Emma's reaction. She looks so offended and confused.

"What's going on here?" I turn to see Alessio standing above me and Emma.

"Daddy, the baby kicked me," Emma pouts.

"Did he?" Alessio fakes anger and plays with Emma.

"He did. I don't want a brother. Boys are bad. I want a sister. Can I have a sister instead?" She screams in excitement at the thought of a sister.

Alessio picks Emma up in his arms. "Maybe next time."

Next time? There's no next time. I'm already exhausted from carrying this one. Not to mention the literal hell I've been through. If Alessio thinks I'm going to have another baby he's out of his mind.

Greta walks into the living room. "Do you need me to stay tonight, Mr. Vitale?"

Alessio puts Emma back on the ground. "No, we're good. Go home, Greta."

Greta nods and makes her exit.

Emma walks over to her puzzle and continues to fiddle with the puzzle pieces.

Alessio comes around the couch and lifts my feet and sits down and places my feet on top of his lap. "How are you feeling?"

I don't know how to answer that. I still feel the pain from all I have been through, but the good memories of Damien have suppressed it temporarily for now. "Better."

"I actually wanted to ask you something. Next week, one of my underbosses is having a Thanksgiving dinner party. I was hoping you would come along with me."

I'm stunned that Alessio wants me to go out with him. Even though we are married, I assumed I would be kept here at home while he went out.

That is what my papa did. Kept me at home like some prize, never allowed me to go out and mingle with people.

Despite my injuries and being pregnant, I don't want to miss this opportunity to go out. And considering today has been better, I think going out would help even more.

"I would love that," I meekly say.

Alessio smiles. "Great, I will have a stylist bring some outfits here next week for you to pick out."

I'm about to ask more about the party when Emma throws her puzzle piece in frustration at the wall.

Alessio shakes his head in disapproval. "I guess someone is ready for bed." He gets up and picks Emma up. "Let's go." Emma pouts as Alessio carries her upstairs.

Once they are gone, I can't help but feel an emptiness.

CHAPTER 23

Anna

I woke up once again in Alessio's arms. I'm not sure how I got there considering we went to sleep on our own sides last night.

It seemed to happen multiple times the last several nights in the last week.

I don't bother trying to wiggle out of his grasp since I'm in a good mood again today after having another great dream about my brothers.

I realize if I focus on the good, the bad memories fade and with it the pain. It's only temporary as the bad always comes blasting in but I don't let it deter me.

I spent the morning with Emma and the afternoon trying on different outfits a stylist had brought in.

My bump made the majority of the dresses I tried on look utterly unflattering.

I felt like a blimp, and I still have 3 more months to go.

The last dress I tried on was a long silver satin dress with a slit up to my thigh that molded around my curves including my bump perfectly. Emma thought I looked like a princess as well, so I decided on the last dress.

I did my hair in soft waves and kept my makeup natural. I also got my cast removed from my hand allowing me to finally scratch an itch I've been dying to scratch for days.

Despite my swollen feet, I force myself to wear strappy silver heels. I'm sure I will regret it tomorrow morning but I'm too excited about being able to go out to a party for once.

The only parties I was allowed to go to were the ones my papa had at the house. And I was only allowed for a short period before I was forced to go to my bedroom for the remainder of the party.

I check on Emma who is playing in her room with Greta to make sure she has everything she needs before heading downstairs. She seems to be doing well so I make my way downstairs.

Alessio and Carter are waiting downstairs. Not sure who is more shocked. Alessio or Carter. Maybe they thought I would be a ball of a mess considering everything that has happened the last several weeks. Some days I'm surprised I'm not.

Alessio walks up to me and gives me a kiss on the cheek. "You look beautiful."

A shiver runs down my spine. I didn't expect that. "Thank you." I can feel my cheeks getting warm.

"Should we go?" Carter asks.

Alessio nods and puts his hand on my lower back and guides me towards the elevator.

Once in the elevator, I look at Alessio from the corner of my eye. I can't figure him out.

When we first married, I was afraid of him. After how our wedding night went, that fear increased.

Now I don't fear him anymore. I know he would never hurt me. In fact, he saved me from Ronan. He has been kind and patient with me. But I don't know where we stand.

We get to the party that is being held outside the city at one of the underbosses' home. It is a large mansion in a gated community. Of course, it's not comparable to Papa's but it's still a beautiful house. If anything, it felt more of a home than my own home ever did.

We are greeted by the underboss Thomas and his wife Zita at the door. They are kind and welcoming. It could be an act since Alessio is Thomas' boss, but I still appreciated the kindness.

Alessio guided me into the living room where all the guests were mingling and having drinks. Once we entered, the room went dead silent. It reminded me of when I went to Adrian Russo's wake. I guess this is something I have to get used to.

After a few seconds, several guests came up and greeted Alessio and introduced themselves to me. They all seemed nice. Some of the men gawked which made me feel uncomfortable and reminded me of Sergai. But it didn't last long since Alessio would give them a look and they would quickly excuse themselves in fear. One man looked like his eyes were going to fall out of his sockets out of fear when Alessio gave him a deadly glare. It made me chuckle at watching people run in fear, but Alessio did not find it amusing at all.

I'm just finishing up having a conversation with one of the captain's wives when I smell a head-spinning fragrance. Before I even turn, I know Gia is around.

Gia walks over to me and Alessio with a wine glass in her head. She is wearing a blue dress with a very low neckline that is barely holding her tits in.

The most shocking part is her lips. They look like two giant sausages. I'm sure she had them done since the last time I saw her.

"Anna, I'm surprised you came today. Considering everything."

"Everything?" I ask.

"I wouldn't have the courage to get out of bed let alone come to the party after being kidnapped and tortured by the Irish." Gia gives a badly mocked pitied look.

"I wouldn't have the courage to come to a party dressed like a whore," Alessio interjects to mine and Gia's shock.

Gia's face morphs into anger but she doesn't say a word. She knows she can't say anything to Alessio.

"Well excuse me." She turns and leaves, smacking her heels a little too loudly with each step.

"Ignore her, she's just mad because I had Nico cancel her cards after her last interaction with you. Apparently, she had to sell her old designer bags to pay for her plastic surgery."

"Clearly she didn't make a lot off her bags because it looks like she went to a cheap doctor," I comment. Alessio bursts into laughter.

People around us seem surprised and are gawking like we are some rare commodity. I didn't mean to make a joke, but Gia's surgery does not look good.

I notice Gia and Nico in the corner of the room. She seems to be saying something to him, but he just shrugs and takes a drink. She looks like she's going to burst in the middle of the room right there, but instead she storms off in anger.

Nico notices me staring and comes towards us.

"Is everything okay?" I ask. I don't want to be the reason things are bad between Nico and Gia. Alessio had previously told me that Nico hates Gia, but I don't want to add gasoline to an already fueling fire.

Nico grins. "Everything is great. Gia just left. Makes my night a hell of a lot easier."

I shake my head at Nico. His marriage is a mess and I hate that they hate each other and are stuck in a miserable marriage.

Alessio grabs my hand. "Let's go eat." I smile and follow his lead.

Alessio

It's nearing midnight and Anna is exhausted. She didn't say anything throughout the party, but I could tell she was having a hard time staying awake. Even though the party was still going on, I decided to call it a night.

Nico decided to leave with us and Carter since Gia took his car and left hours before.

Nico still had a blast though and at one point he disappeared with one of the waitresses for half an hour. Usually, I would give Nico hell for cheating on his wife at a family party, but Gia is a bitch.

Gia seems to have something against Anna. She must hate at the end of the day she is no longer the highest-ranking wife in the family, not to mention everyone seems to genuinely like Anna.

Anna fell asleep as soon as we got into the SUV. Her head is resting on my lap as I play with her soft golden blonde hair. She looks angelic and peaceful as she sleeps.

We are driving past a secluded wooded area when Carter, who is driving all of a sudden speeds up. "We have a problem."

Nico, who is sitting in the passenger seat, turns and looks through the back windows. "Shit, we have at least two dark SUVs following us."

I pull my gun from the gun holster while trying not to wake Anna. "Where are the guards?"

Nico pulls out his phone and starts to dial. "Calling them now."

One of the black SUVs slams into the back of our car. Carter swerves off the road and back on again.

Our security guards' SUV comes from behind and shoots at the unknown SUV. Shots are fired between the two SUVs until the second unknown SUV slams into our security guards SUV sending them flying into a ditch.

Nico rolls down his window and motions for Carter to switch lanes and fires shots at the first unknown SUV, hitting their tire causing it to tumble to its side.

The second unknown SUV speeds up and fires back. Luckily our SUV is bulletproof and doesn't get through.

Anna stirs from the noise and tries to get up. I push her down. "No stay down." She goes stiff but stays down.

The unknown SUV fires another round of shots and hits one of our tires.

Carter turns into a wooden area. "We have to get out and run. The tire is going to give in any second now."

Nico checks his phone. "No phone service in this area. I'll try and make a diversion while you guys run."

"No! You are coming with us!" I shout.

"Don't worry, I'll be right behind you." Nico winks. "You get Anna to safety."

I want to argue but I have to make sure Anna is safe.

The SUV begins to slow down. Carter slams the breaks. "Now. Run!"

I grab Anna's hand and pull her out of the SUV and we start to run towards the woods.

I hear shots being fired and look back and see Nico firing at the unknown SUV.

I can feel Anna's trembling hand in mine, but we can't stop now. We continue to run for a few minutes until we hear a twig break behind us. Carter quickly turns and aims at the noise.

Nico puts his hands up in mock surrender. "Just me."

Carter puts his gun down and rolls his eyes. "Did you get them?"

Nico shakes his head. "No, I got a few but I heard one of them call for backup."

"Fuck!" I swear.

"There is something else." Nico pauses and looks at Anna. "They were Russian."

Anna goes pale. "Why would Bratva attack us? Didn't you have an alliance with my papa?"

Nico, Carter, and I share a look. This doesn't seem like the time to tell Anna her father had planned on double-crossing us and taking our child to raise while she is tossed to Sergai the creep like some toy.

We hear another twig break. I push Anna behind me and the three of us pull out our weapons. We can't figure out where the noise came from. Then another twig breaks. Leaves rustling under boots.

Shit. It's multiple boots.

"Surrender and hand over Anna." Ivan walks out from behind a tree. A few seconds later a group of men walk out from different hidden areas. We are surrounded.

"This is war," Nico seethes. "You are going to die for this."

Ivan laughs. "The only person who is going to die is you. Put down your guns and surrender."

If we surrender, they will kill us and take Anna.

Ivan motions for the men surrounding us to move when shots are fired, killing several of the Russian men. A shot from an unknown location hits Ivan. Carter, Nico, and I shoot the remaining Russian men still standing.

We turn towards Ivan who is now on the ground bleeding. He is clutching his chest when a man with blonde hair and piercing blue eyes comes out from behind the tree and points the gun at Ivan's head.

Ivan shakes and begs the man who without a single shred of emotion pulls the trigger.

Anna takes a step forward and I put my arm around the top of her bump and pull her towards me.

"Maxim?" Anna sobs.

The blonde man looks up and stares at Anna and then her bump. I feel the need to protect Anna and our baby.

"It's been a while, Malyshka. You've changed," says Maxim without any emotion.

"What are you doing here?" Anna again tries to take a step forward, but I keep her pressed to me.

I don't trust this guy and if this is her brother Maxim, the stories I've heard about him are unsettling, to say the least.

"You need to go. More of Papa's men are coming. They will be coming from the north side of the woods. There is a road a few miles east with a gas station. Head that way."

"How can we trust you?" I ask.

Maxim takes a step forward and I can see from the corner of my eyes Nico and Carter have their weapons up.

Maxim doesn't display any reaction or emotion. We hear noises from the north. "They're here. Go now." Maxim turns and heads towards the noise.

Anna is shaking in my arms. I turn to my brothers. "Let's go."

We head east.

CHAPTER 24

Alessio

O nce we arrived at the road, Nico was able to get a signal and call back up.

We arrive back at the penthouse and Anna heads straight upstairs to the bedroom. She hasn't said a word since we left the woods.

Nico steps in front of me. "This isn't good. Maxim is a known sociopath. He stabbed his own pregnant girlfriend over a dozen times."

"I know." It's why I got so protective of Anna back in the woods. She is pregnant and Maxim clearly has no problem hurting pregnant women.

"Why do you think he's back? And what was he doing there tonight? How did he even find us?" Carter questions.

"The bracelet." Realization passes through me. The bracelet with the tracking chip Dima had told us about.

"You need to get rid of that bracelet," Nico states.

"Let's discuss this tomorrow morning. Go rest for now," I say to my brothers.

They nod and head towards the elevator.

Carter turns to Nico. "I'm assuming you're staying at my place."

Nico throws his arm around Carter's neck and smiles. "Of course, where else would I want to be?"

I shake my head at my brothers and head upstairs to my wife.

Anna

Maxim is back. A couple of days ago when I thought I saw Maxim, I thought I was imagining things. It couldn't possibly be him. But now I don't know. Maybe it was him. Watching me from a distance. What is he doing back? Does he know why Papa wanted to kill us? Where has he been? Why did he leave?

I have so many questions I need answers to. I decide I can't wait.

I quickly change into a pair of leggings, a top, and boots. I am just about to leave when Alessio walks into the bedroom.

He looks at my outfit. "Where are you going?"

"I need to speak to Maxim." I try to head towards the door, but Alessio blocks me.

"It's past midnight. And how do you even know where your brother is?" He gives me a questioning look. "Do you know where your brother is?"

"No, but I'll figure it out." I know that I probably sound illogical. I can't possibly go around the entire city searching for him but I can't sit around and wait either.

Alessio doesn't move so I try to go around him, but he grabs me and picks me up like a doll.

"You're not going anywhere. You are pregnant and your father just attacked us. It's not safe." He puts me down on the bed.

"That's why I need to go. I need to find out why my papa would attack us." I try to get up from the bed, but Alessio pushes me down by the shoulders.

"I already know," he says.

"You know?"

Alessio sighs. "It's late. How about we talk about this tomorrow morning?"

"No, let's talk now."

"No, tomorrow morning."

I want to argue and talk now but I know Alessio won't have a conversation now. He seems to be hell-bent on me resting. I nod in agreement and change into my nightie and crawl back into bed.

It's not until I'm in bed do I realize how exhausted I am.

Alessio joins me a few minutes later and pulls me towards him like he has done the last couple of nights.

I face up towards Alessio. "I'm not going to jump or kill myself while you're sleeping. If that's what you think."

Alessio's body goes rigid. "What makes you think I think that?"

"Since that night, you always pull me into you. As if you're trying to cage me in so I can't run away."

Alessio loosens his grip around me but doesn't let me go. "That night," he starts. "You scared the shit out of me. I thought I was going to lose you and the baby. I tried to hold on to you so you wouldn't try something like that again. But since then, I have only done it because it seems help with your nightmares."

"Oh," is all I can say. I'm astounded.

I didn't realize Alessio could tell I was having nightmares so often. I think back to the last time I had one and realize since waking up in Alessio's arms I haven't had one.

"Go to sleep now." Alessio yawns.

I place my head on Alessio's warm chest and close my eyes.

CHAPTER 25

Anna

I t's early morning and I make my way downstairs to get breakfast. As I get to the bottom of the steps Emma bounces towards me, almost knocking me out.

"Emma, you can't jump on your mom like that. It's not good for the baby," Alessio cautions. He pulls Emma away from me and picks her up. "Are you okay?"

"I'm fine," I reassure. I'm doing better than I have in days. Despite my papa trying to kill us and my brother's sudden appearance last night. I didn't have any nightmares again and I'm starting to think it may be due to Alessio.

For the longest time, I was alone but now I feel like I have someone. A family. Someone to comfort me and be there for me. "Can we talk about last night?" I ask Alessio.

He frowns but puts Emma down. "Emma, why don't you get Greta to make you pancakes?"

Emma grins, "Okay!" and runs towards the kitchen.

"Let's talk in my office." Alessio motions for me to follow him.

Once in his office, he guides me towards the couch at the side.

I take a seat beside Alessio and don't give him a chance to try and come up with some excuse to not tell me. "I need to know why my papa would want to kill us and why my brother has returned."

Alessio rubs the back of his neck. "I don't know why Maxim is back but in regards to Yuri, I didn't want to tell you considering he is your father."

"What didn't you want to tell me?" I know I won't like what Alessio is going to tell me already. Knowing my papa, he is up to no good.

Alessio sighs. "Remember previously I had told you Dima, your father's enforcer, had contacted us to give us information? Well, according to him, your father planned on killing me after you had our son and taking him and raising him as the heir to the Vitale family."

I'm not surprised Papa had plans to take my child from me. He only cares about power and my son could gain him power. But I wouldn't ever allow him to take my child and use him. I would die fighting for my child.

Alessio looks concerned and touches my hand lightly. "Anna, are you okay?"

I nod. "I've already known my papa only cared about power. I'm not surprised. But I wouldn't let him take my child from me or use him for his own gain."

"According to Dima, your father already made a deal with Sergai, for him to have you after I'm dead," he seethes in disgust.

I've known for years Sergai has an interest in me. It started when I was fifteen years old, and he always made me uncomfortable with the way he leers at me. I'm sure he had suggested for me to be given to him after Papa kills Alessio.

"You don't look surprised to hear that either," Alessio mentions.

"No, Sergai has always been a creep around me."

"This is my fault," Alessio groans and rubs his eyes with his hand.

I don't understand how my papa wanting to kill him and Sergai being a creep is his fault. He must see the uncertain look on my face and takes both my hands into his.

Now looking at our hands, mine are so small compared to his large ones.

"I caused you to fear me from the start of our marriage and of course, you didn't trust me to tell me about them."

I'm thrown off at Alessio's statement. I did fear him in the beginning, but I now know it wasn't his fault. It was my papa's. It may have been Ivan who drugged Alessio, but I am sure it was on my papa's orders. And now that I know he had plans to kill him, I'm positive it was part of his great big plan.

My lack of trust in Alessio is due to what I've gone through in the past. I've been wary of everyone since Damien's death.

Despite it all, Alessio has gained my trust.

"I do trust you," I confess. "You saved me and Emma when we were kidnapped."

"I'm to be blamed for you being kidnapped and tortured."

"No, you're not. You do not control the actions of others." I give Alessio an encouraging smile to know I don't blame him for anything.

He looks surprised but swiftly smiles back. "We can't keep any more secrets from one another. For the sake of our child."

"Children," I interrupt.

Alessio's brows furrowed in confusion. "Children?"

"Emma is my child too. She may not be my child by blood, but I love her nonetheless and would die for her. I will love her no less than my son."

Alessio smiles widely. "I know you would. You protected her and kept her safe. No more secrets."

Alessio

Anna looks extra beautiful today. She is wearing a white long sleeve dress and has her soft golden blonde hair is straight today.

She looks at me with those ocean blue eyes. "No more secrets. Is there anything else?"

"I need your bracelet." I point to her wrist with the bracelet on it.

"Why?"

"It has a tracker on it. I think that's how your brother Maxim found us last night."

Anna looks down at her bracelet and plays with the little snowflakes, "No, you can't have it," she whispers.

"Anna," I warn.

"How do you even know it has a tracker?" she questions.

"When you and Emma were kidnapped, Dima had told us about it. It's how we found you."

Anna's eyes start to fill with tears. "You can't have it."

I get up from my seat and crouch in front of Anna while holding her hands into mine. Her skin is soft and pale compared to my rough and tanned skin. "It's for your safety."

She pulls her hands out of mine and shakes her head. "No, my brother gave it to me. You can't have it," she repeats.

"Maxim?"

"No, my brother Damien." Her voice is laced with pain.

"The one who died under mysterious circumstances?"

Anna scoffs. "Mysterious circumstances? My brother was killed by my papa." Anna's voice is filled with hatred. Hatred towards her father.

"How do you know this?" I ask.

"Because I was there." She pauses for a few seconds before continuing. "Two years ago, my brother Damien fell in love with a waitress named Eva that worked at one of Papa's restaurants. He wanted to get out of this line of business and decided he and Eva were going to run away together."

"What happened?" I ask lightly, hoping not to scare her into closing herself off again.

"He asked me to go with him. A chance to be free from Papa and I said yes. He gave me this bracelet saying he would find me no matter where I was. The night we were supposed to leave, I was going to meet Damien outside the gates. He had everything planned. I just needed to meet him. But I messed up. While I was trying to leave, I ran into Ivan. He always used to be nice to me and pretended to be my friend for years. My brothers warned me not to trust him, but I foolishly told him Damien's plan. I trusted him. Thinking I was saying goodbye to a friend. He went straight to my papa and told him. My papa killed Damien for his betrayal."

Anna begins to shake at her recalling of the past. I hold her in my arms and soothe her and she grasps my shirt into her fists.

"Your father didn't kill you?"

She shakes her head. "No, he gave me a choice. Either throw the blame on my brother by calling him a traitor and live or admit my betrayal and die. I blamed my brother," she croaks.

I can't believe Yuri would do that to his own children.

"He let me live but I wasn't allowed outside the house after that. You can't have the bracelet. It's all I have from Damien," Anna says in so much pain.

I pull back. "Okay, you can keep it."

She sniffles, "I can?"

"Yeah, you can. Why don't you go and have breakfast with Emma? I have some things I need to take care of."

She nods and gets up and heads towards the door but stops and turns around. "Alessio, my papa can't have our son."

"He won't," I affirm.

CHAPTER 26

Alessio

I'm working from home today. With Ronan still out there and now Yuri declaring war, I need to be close to my family.

Nico is working on his laptop on the couch in my office when Carter walks in.

"I've been trying to get the scope around town and apparently word is we killed the Russians after they attacked us. No mention of Maxim." Carter takes a seat in front of my desk.

Nico closes his laptop. "Anna previously said that her brothers hate Yuri. Maybe they're secretly starting a coup?"

"Maybe but we can't take any chances. We need to have our guard up," I tell my brothers.

Nico gets up from his spot and walks over to me and Carter. "Did you talk to Anna about Maxim?"

"No."

"Did you take her bracelet?"

"No."

Nico furrows his brows, "Why not?"

"You need to take her bracelet. As long as she has it, her location will be known to anyone with information on it," Carter states.

"Her brother Damien gave it to her before he died." I fill my brothers in on what Anna told me about Damien's death. I could tell Anna feels guilty for blaming her brother to save herself, but if she didn't, she too would be dead right now. Damien was already dead. There was no saving him.

"Shit, that's fucked. No wonder his kids are all so messed up," Nico remarks.

I know we are stretched in resources and men dealing with the Irish and now Bratva. We can't fight two wars at the same time. "For now, let's keep an eye out for Maxim but our main priority is still finding Ronan. As for Yuri and the bratva, Anna and Emma won't be leaving the penthouse anymore. It will prevent Yuri from getting his hands on them."

Nico and Carter head out and I go to find Anna and Emma.

I find Anna in Emma's bed with Emma snuggled into her side sleeping. Anna has one arm around Emma and the other on her growing belly.

When Anna said Emma was her child too, it made me ecstatic. I worried about the dynamics once Anna has the baby.

I know she would still love and care for Emma, but Emma is still not hers by blood. I know plenty of people who claim they would never differentiate between their own blood children but of course, they have favorites.

Anna saying Emma is just as much her child as our unborn son only solidified her love for Emma.

I pull the blanket over both my girls and close the door and leave to allow them to rest.

Anna

I told Alessio about Damien and his death. I have held onto the pain for so long and, besides my brothers, have not told anyone. My brothers all said I was not to be blamed but I knew they were saying it out of love for me.

They are much older than me and babied me growing up. Losing Damien was the most heart-wrenching experience in my life. He wanted to save me and asked me to come with him.

I made the foolish mistake to trust Ivan thinking he was a friend. Instead, he was someone looking for an opportunity to get ahead and he found it when I told him about Damien's plan. My papa rewarded him by promoting him within the bratva. And I lost my brother.

After that I never trusted anyone again, until now.

With Damien gone, each of my brothers fell into turmoil and lost their ways. Everyone including Alessio and his brothers calls them monsters and they might be to everyone else. But to me, they are my brothers who raised me and protected me.

For the longest time, I blamed myself for not only Damien's death but my brothers leaving.

When Alessio blamed himself for Ronan and my papa's action's I realized I knew how he felt. But he wasn't to blame. When everyone said the same to me, I never believed them but now I know. The only ones to blame are the ones who are responsible for that night.

Ivan, who betrayed me, is now dead, thanks to Maxim. My papa who pulled the trigger, who I know if Alessio doesn't kill, my brothers will one day. Their hatred for my father has no limits. Then there is Ronan, who kidnapped and tortured me. He was also willing to do the same to a three-year-old child. Alessio said he would kill him for what he did, and I don't doubt that for a second.

I pull Christmas decorations out of boxes with Emma. Christmas is only a few weeks away.

Emma is in a corner throwing tinsel around herself saying it's magic. I pull out some ornaments from a box but don't like the color selection.

It's all bright pink and silver. They were most likely picked out by Maria, Alessio's first wife.

I had hoped for a red and gold classic tree. But Alessio has put me and Emma on lock down.

With Ronan and now my papa out there trying to kill us, he doesn't want to take any chances. I could tell he thought I was going to argue about it, but I've lived my entire life locked away. A few weeks is nothing.

Besides, I had Emma to keep me busy.

I put the ornaments back into the box and head towards the kitchen. Greta is cooking up a feast like she always does.

The smell makes my stomach growl. "This smells amazing."

Greta looks up and smiles. "I hope you would like it. You are not gaining enough weight." She points with the wooden spoon towards my stomach.

I roll my eyes at Greta. She thinks I'm too skinny for a pregnant woman, but the doctor assured me the baby is healthy and is getting all the nutrients he needs.

It just so happens the baby is taking on all the fat. The doctor was surprised at the large size of the baby. Considering how tall Alessio is, I'm not surprised our son is big.

"Greta, are there any more Christmas decorations? I was hoping for more of a classic look."

Greta puts down the wooden spoon and rubs her hands on her apron. "Maria loved pink, so all her decorations were that color. But I can have one of the guards go out and pick some things up."

"Please, if you could? I don't usually mind pink but this much pink is going to make this place look like Barbie's house," I laugh.

I'm not being dramatic, there really is way too much pink. I can see why Maria and Gia were friends. They seemed to have similar tastes.

I've always wondered what Alessio and Maria's relationship was like but never had the courage to ask Alessio.

I decide to take my chance and ask Greta. "Greta, what was Maria like?"

Greta hesitates for a second. "She was different."

"Different?" I'm not sure what she means by that.

Greta shuts off the stove and puts the dirty dishes in the sink. "She was fickle and materialistic. She was similar to Gia but not as rude."

"How was Alessio's and Maria's relationship?"

"They were friends before they married and continued to be friends after. Rather than husband and wife they were more friends than anything else."

I'm curious to know more about the dynamics between the two but I know the only person who would know is Alessio. No one knows what goes on behind closed doors.

"Why don't you go and rest? I will get the guards to bring over some new decorations soon."

"Okay." I smile and head back to the family room.

Only there is no resting for me. Emma has tangled a number of tinsel strings into her hair like gum.

"How did you do this?" I try and pull on the shiny strings out of her hair and she just shrugs in complete cluelessness.

I spend the next hour trying to pull out the tinsel from Emma's hair without hurting her. It's a challenge considering it's tied around her hair pretty well.

It would be easier to get gum out of her hair than this. Once I'm done the guards have brought up new Christmas decorations in a number of boxes.

I go through each one and I'm pleased with the color choices. There is a box with tinsel which I take out and throw away as soon as it caught Emma's eye. I don't need a repeat of earlier. She pouts at first but gets over it quickly to help me decorate the tree.

Alessio

I get home to find the entire place decorated for Christmas. Unlike previous years the entire penthouse is decorated in red and gold colors. It makes the place feel homey and warm.

I head upstairs to find Anna already passed out in bed. She is wearing a two-piece silk camisole and short sleep set. Her stomach is peeking out from her top, showing her growing belly.

In the last several weeks it has grown tremendously. I assume it has to do with Greta filling Anna's plate with enormous amounts of food.

I quickly shower and change and get into bed and pull Anna into me. It has become a routine for me now and it seems to help her as well.

As soon as I'm about to close the lights I feel a slight kick to my side. The baby is kicking again. Anna unconsciously rubs her hand on her stomach in her sleep. The baby kicks again and Anna frowns in her sleep.

"Stop that," I say to the baby as I rub Anna's stomach to try and ease the baby. Instead, the baby kicks twice as hard, even shocking me at the strong impact. Anna grumbles in her sleep and wakes up.

She squints at me and then at the clock. "What time is it?"

"1 am."

She moans in annoyance. "He's been doing this all day. That and playing with my bladder like it's some toy."

I laugh at Anna's expense, which she does not like.

She smacks me on the chest. "You try peeing multiple times an hour throughout the day." She flips over clearly annoyed at me and closes her eyes. I pull her towards me again and she glares at me. "If you laugh again, I will push this baby out right here and now and you can take care of it."

Her annoyance is cute, and I try not to smile knowing she might actually deliver the baby right here in anger.

"Okay." I kiss her on the top of her forehead and turn off the lights.

Within seconds she falls asleep, but the baby continues to kick, clearly not ready to sleep. After a while the baby finally stops, allowing everyone to finally rest.

CHAPTER 27

Anna

It's snowing and the city looks beautiful. It's covered in a beautiful white blanket and the windows are cold to the touch.

Emma is pressed against the window looking outside. She had asked if we can go out and play at the park but with Papa and Ronan still out there it's not safe.

I can tell she was disappointed but I had promised her we could build our own fort inside. Her sad expression pierced my heart. I out of all people know what it feels like to be trapped inside and not allowed to go out.

I don't want that for Emma, but I can't risk her safety either.

Christmas is around the corner, and it has been weeks since Papa attacked.

Being the wife of a Capo, I was invited to several important parties and events that I had to politely decline as well.

Emma pulls herself away from the window and walks over to the couch and lays down with her head buried down into the cushions.

I can see her little body shaking and I walk over to her and stroke the top of her head. "My love, what's wrong?"

"I want to go outside," she cries into the cushion.

"We can have more fun inside," I try to persuade her.

"No! It's not the same." She raises her head and there is snot coming down her nose and her face is drenched in tears.

I try to figure out an excuse or even a bribe at this point to make her stop crying.

Emma is a child, and she doesn't understand why she can't go outside. She isn't aware of the dangers, and she shouldn't have to be. I would not want her to live in fear.

"Emma," I start but a penetrating pain goes up my back. I fold over in pain and grab onto the coffee table.

Emma sees me and gets up quickly from the couch and runs towards the kitchen. Hopefully to get Greta.

The pain doesn't stop, and I feel a liquid between my legs. At first, I think I may have peed myself considering how often I had to run to the bathroom lately but look down to see it's dark red.

Alarm bells are going off in my head. My baby. Something's wrong.

The pain increases and I can't hold it in anymore and scream in pain.

Greta runs towards me. "Anna!" She grabs her phone from her pocket and dials a number. She says something to someone on the phone, but I can't understand. The pain is deafening. I can't think or do anything. A few minutes later, I hear the elevator ring and two guards come in. One picks me up and I'm carried into the elevator.

Alessio

I got the call that Anna was rushed to the hospital.

Nico and I get there to find out Anna has the same clumsy doctor as last time. He is capable at his job and based on the credentials, he finished at the top of his program in medical school but his fear of me is annoying.

Most of the time I prefer people to be afraid of me but not the doctor who may have to make life and death decisions about my wife and son.

"Mr. Vitale," the doctor murmurs while looking at the ground. "Your wife has gone into premature labor."

"How could this happen?" I shout. Anna is almost 8 months but it's too early to have the baby now.

The doctor flinches and his shoulders hunch inwards, "This can happen due to stress throughout the pregnancy or other reasons." The doctor doesn't look up and continues to talk to the floor. "Your wife was rushed into surgery and is being treated by a specialist. They will have news for you soon."

Nico's jaw ticks. "Can you look the fuck up instead of staring at the ground?"

The doctor instantly raises his head but doesn't meet our eyes. "Are there any other questions?"

"What are the chances of the baby...." I don't finish the sentence.

"Dr. Keller is the top neonatal surgeon on the east coast. Your wife and child are in good hands."

I nod at the doctor who takes this cue to speed walk away. I take a seat in the waiting room as Nico makes some calls in the hallway.

Nico returns. "Good news, the quack doctor wasn't lying about Dr. Keller. He's good."

I don't respond. Nico takes a seat next to me. "It's going to be okay."

"Is it?" I ask. "Yuri wants his hands on my son and Ronan is still out there."

"I will take care of Ronan. I give you my word. For everything he has put you, Anna, and Emma, through," Nico promises. "You take care of your family."

A doctor in blue scrubs comes out. "Mr. Vitale?"

I get up from my seat. "Is my wife okay?"

The doctor smiles. "She's fine and so is your son. We currently have him in the NICU so we can monitor him but both mother and baby are healthy."

I shake the doctor's hand and thank him. Both Anna and our son are okay.

CHAPTER 28

Anna

I open my eyes to an annoying beeping sound. The room is white and unfamiliar.

I look around and realize I'm at the hospital. I feel my stomach but don't feel the baby. I quickly get up which was the wrong thing to do as a horrible pain pulsates through my body.

"Be careful." I turn and see Alessio at the doorway and in his arms is a bundle of fabric with what looks like a baby peeking from the top.

"Is that?" I can't finish my sentence.

Alessio walks over to my bed. "It's our son." He gently passes the baby into my arms.

He's beautiful. He's small and has the cutest button nose and small little lips. He has dark brown hair like Alessio. He's sleeping so I can't tell what color his eyes are but I'm sure they will be perfect like the rest of him. All throughout my pregnancy all he did was kick and play in my belly and now he is sleeping.

I look up at Alessio. "What happened? I still had 1 and a half months left."

"The doctor thinks due to stress throughout your pregnancy it caused you to go into premature labor."

"I'm sorry," I apologize. Not sure for what. Maybe out of habit.

Alessio is also thrown off by my apology. "It's not your fault. If it's anyone's fault it's –"

"My papa's and Ronan's," I interject. I don't want Alessio blaming himself again. "Where's Emma?"

"She's at home. I didn't think it's safe for her to come here yet. I actually plan on moving both of you as soon as all the equipment we might need is set up at home."

I nod in understanding. I also want to be home. For once I found a home where I'm safe and happy. There is nowhere I would rather be.

Alessio gets a text and scowls at his phone. "I'll be right back." He gives me a kiss on the forehead that sends a weird feeling in my heart and walks out of the room. I know whatever he received isn't good but for now, me and my son are safe and happy right here.

Alessio

I get a text from Nico advising Yuri and Sergai have shown up at the hospital.

I walk out to find Nico standing in the hallway outside of Anna's room with a number of our guards across from Yuri, Sergai, and their guards.

"What do you want?" I glare at Yuri. I could kill him right here and now but a shootout outside Anna's room is not the best option.

"I came to see my daughter and grandson." Yuri smiles like a shark.

"She wants nothing to do with you and since your attack on us, our alliance is over," I remind Yuri.

Sergai licks his lips. "How is Anna? I heard she had to have emergency surgery? I hope she is still able to bear more children. I have always wanted an heir myself." Sergai's eyes are of a predator. I want to rip them out with my knife.

I take a step forward and the Russians pull out their guns and in response so do my men. I hear people screaming in the background, but my eyes are locked on Yuri and Sergai.

Yuri raises his hand to his guards. "You have until the end of the week to hand over my daughter and grandson to me or I will burn down your entire damn building. If I can't have them, no one can." Yuri takes a step back and motions for his men to follow suit. They all back away and leave.

I turn to my brother. "We need to move Anna and the baby now."

Nico pulls out his phone and begins making calls to make the arrangements.

CHAPTER 29

Anna

I was moved out of the hospital a few hours after I woke up with the baby.

When I arrived back at the penthouse it was late evening.

Alessio had the downstairs guest bedroom set up with every possible equipment I or the baby might need.

Dr. Watson is also on standby staying at Nico's guestroom below our floor in case there is an emergency.

I heard Gia had a fit about it, but I don't care too much. She didn't even come to congratulate or see the baby at the hospital. Not even now that the baby was back home.

I know she doesn't like me but mine and Alessio's son is now her nephew.

I'm sitting on the bed with the baby in my arms trying to get him to burp. The nurses at the hospital gave me instructions on how to feed, burp, change, and bathe the baby quickly. I didn't have much time to learn or ask questions since Alessio wanted us back at the penthouse as soon as possible.

I continue to rub the baby's back in circles as the nurses taught me but the baby isn't burping.

Alessio walks in. "What's wrong?"

"I can't get the baby to burp."

"Here." Alessio moves forward and picks the baby up in his arms and lays him against his chest. He makes circles on the baby's back and within seconds the baby burps.

"How did you do that?"

"I learned from when Emma was a baby."

I didn't realize how hands-on Alessio was with Emma. Most men prefer to have nannies or their wives take care of the children. That's what my papa did anyway.

"We need to name him," I point out.

"What names did you have in mind?"

"Since he is going to be the heir of the Vitale Family, it seems only right to give him an Italian name. Maybe something like Daniele?"

Alessio smiles. "I like Daniele."

"Do you not have any names in mind?"

"Nope, I like Daniele. I think it suits him." Alessio rocks baby Daniele in his arms.

"Yeah, I think so too." I smile.

CHAPTER 30

Alessio

I t's been 5 days since Anna had Daniele. She and the baby have been doing great.

Emma is over the moon at having a little brother, despite her insistence she wants a baby sister.

I'm working in my office when I get a call from Nico. I answer it right away. "Is everything okay?"

There is a pause on the other end of the call for a second. "Not sure, depends." I don't like the sound of this. Nico continues, "Yuri is dead."

I stand up from my chair. "How?"

"Nikolai Petrov returned ,and with his brother Maxim, he killed Yuri and a number of other loyalists to Yuri last night."

"What about Sergai?"

"He got away, but Nikolai has a hit out on him." There is silence on both ends. Yuri's death is a good thing but now with him dead, Nikolai will be taking over.

I have heard rumors of the vicious and out-of-control Petrov brothers for years. Him as the new leader of the bratva may not be a good thing.

"Are you going to tell Anna?" Nico asks.

"I have to." He was her father after all. "Let's set up a meeting between us and our underbosses. We can't have them doubting our strength and control of the situation. Find out more information if you can as well."

"I will keep you updated," Nico says before we hang up.

I'm not sure what to tell Anna. I know she hates her father, but he was still her father. Not to mention the sudden appearance of her brothers.

Anna

I've moved back upstairs to my bedroom last night. I hated staying in the guest bedroom downstairs. It didn't feel right for some reason.

I'm sitting on my bed with the baby on my lap and Emma asleep next to me. She adores Daniele and wants to be with him at all times. I'm sure when they grow up it will be a different story but for now, I'm enjoying their bond.

Alessio opens the door and walks in. He looks concerned. "We need to talk."

"About what?"

"Maybe we should talk outside." He signals with his chin towards Emma and Daniele.

I pick Daniele up and place him in the center of the bed and surround him with pillows, so he won't fall off. I pull a blanket over Emma, grab the baby monitor and turn to Alessio.

His stare is intense and penetrating. I turn around to look at the children thinking I did something wrong but find them comfortably sleeping.

Alessio grabs my hand and pulls me outside and downstairs to the living room. I take a seat on the couch and wait for Alessio to tell me whatever he wanted to talk about.

He makes himself a drink and takes a sip before speaking. "Your father is dead."

I'm blown away by what Alessio has just said. At first, I thought I heard wrong.

I didn't care for my papa, in fact, I hated him and wished he was dead for years but didn't think it was possible. He was too strong and powerful.

"How?" I hear myself ask but my voice feels far away.

"Your brother Nikolai has returned and he along with your other brother Maxim killed him last night."

I knew if anyone would be able to kill Papa it would be my brothers. My papa always feared them and what they became.

"When is his funeral?"

Alessio stops drinking. "Funeral?"

Even if my brothers killed Papa, he was still the Pakhan and would be given a proper funeral. "Can you find out when and where his funeral is?"

Alessio stares at me. "I don't think it's a good idea for you to go to the funeral if there even is one."

"I'm going," I insist. Not for my papa but for my brothers. They will have to be there. Even if they killed him, in our world it would be even more disrespectful if they didn't give Papa a proper funeral and didn't show up.

There is a wailing noise coming from the baby monitor and I realize it's time for Daniele's feeding.

I get up. "Please find out when it is," I say before heading upstairs.

CHAPTER 31

Anna

I t's a cold December day but the sun is out. It's the day of my papa's funeral.

Alessio was able to find out the day and time but I could tell he was against me going.

It didn't matter as I wouldn't have taken no for an answer. I need to be here. Our SUV parks to the side of the cemetery where the funeral is taking place.

I get out and almost trip due to the annoying black veil obstructing my vision. I thought my wedding veil made things hard to see but this one is a hundred times worse.

Alessio grabs my arm to steady me.

I look up at Alessio. "Thank you." I can tell he hates being here, but he still came here for me.

He is always putting me first and catching me when I'm about to fall. A knot forms inside me at the thought of Alessio and how he cares for me.

He gives me a short nod and guides me towards the ceremony.

The winter breeze flows through my open jacket, and I can't help the chill that runs down my body.

Despite the weather, I wore a long-sleeve black dress with knee-high boots and a black jacket. I had hoped the boots would keep me warm, but the breeze just goes up my dress instead.

Nico and Carter are following behind and I can tell they are on their guard. I had told Alessio I was okay going alone but he refused immediately. He doesn't understand I am safe as long as my brothers are nearby.

We get to the gravesite and everyone is speaking in hushed voices in Russian. They are mostly mumbling about how we could show up considering the Italians were just at war with the Russians only a few days ago.

I look around and don't see my brothers anywhere.

Alessio takes me towards the front where we take our seats. Then the hushed voices completely stop. I look to the side and even through the veil I can recognize them anywhere. Nikolai and Maxim.

They walk over to the front and take their seats on the other side. I want to run to them so badly but hold it in.

The minister begins the service as soon as my brothers take their seats. The minister talks about how great my papa is and how much good he has done, and I can't help but roll my eyes.

No one believes these lies. My papa was the worst. He tortured and abused his own children. Killed his own son Damien for wanting to leave. Sold me off to the Italians for power. Despite Alessio not being the monster I thought he was, it doesn't change the fact papa wouldn't have had a problem if he was.

The service ends quickly and dirt is thrown over Papa's coffin. My brothers get up and a swarm of high and low-level bratva members go up to them to give their condolences. More importantly, to win points.

I walk towards them, but Alessio grabs my arm. "We should get going."

"I need to talk to my brothers." I try to pull out of Alessio's grasp but he doesn't budge.

"Anna, it's not safe here in the open. You can talk to your brothers back at the house for the reception."

I nod. "Okay, let's go." I don't want to leave but I can see my brothers at the house. Here in the open may not be the best place to talk in front of everyone.

We arrive at my childhood home after a shore drive.

The three-story mansion where I grew up and lived in hell is still the same.

Once inside the house I can tell Alessio, Nico and Carter are hesitant. They didn't want to come here but again I insisted and they, of course, couldn't let me come here alone.

Once I take my jacket off, I turn to Alessio, "I'll be right back, I just need to use the bathroom." I take a step back and Alessio grips onto my arm again.

"Anna." His voice holds a warning.

"I'll be back in five minutes."

Alessio narrows his eyes. "Okay, five minutes or I'm coming for you."

The look in Alessio's eyes sends a shiver down my spine. Unlike the one from the cold, this one is different.

I head towards the bathroom and walk past it until I get to Papa's office. I stand in front of the large wooden doors. These doors used to scare me growing up, knowing what's to come once I was inside.

"Anna." I turn to the voice and see it's my brother Maxim. I run to give him a hug without a second thought.

"Where did you go?" I croak as my eyes fill with tears I try to hold back.

Maxim strokes my hair gently like he did when I was a child and refused to go to sleep. "Come, Nikolai wants to see you." He pulls me towards Papa's office and opens the door.

Once inside, I notice Nikolai sitting at Papa's desk. His desk now that he is the Pakhan. Nikolai gets up from his desk and walks over towards us. Instantly I run into Nikolai and hug him.

He chuckles. "I guess you missed me."

I want to tell him how much I've missed him, but I can't get the words out. My eyes feel like they are burning from the tears I am holding in.

I refuse to let Nikolai go, afraid this is a dream I will wake up from and he and Maxim will be gone again.

Nikolai hugs me back and just holds me as I continue to refuse to let go. After a few minutes, I release him and pull away. I take in every feature of my brother. His blonde hair and matching blue eyes are still the same but he's aged in the year he has been gone.

My eyes start to fill with tears again. I've missed them so much.

"There's no need to cry anymore, Anna. We're back and no one can hurt you again," Nikolai says.

"What about Alek?" My brother Alek has been in a mental institution for over a year now.

Nikolai pulls away and leans against the desk. "We are going to get him out. First, we have to weed out all of Papa's men. Not to mention finding Sergai." He crosses his arms. "I heard you had a son with the Italian Capo?"

"Yes, my son's name is Daniele. I can't wait for you both to meet him." I smile enthusiastically at Maxim and Nikolai. Maxim doesn't say a word, but I can tell Nikolai is holding something in. "What's wrong?" I ask.

Nikolai comes to stand in front of me and puts his arms on my shoulders. "Nothing. I will take care of everything." I don't get what he means.

Then all of a sudden, the door flies open and Alessio, Nico, and Carter walk in.

Nikolai pushes me behind him. "What do you think you're doing?"

"I'm here for my wife." Alessio holds out his hand for me and I walk towards him. I can see Nikolai's hand twitch, almost in an attempt to stop me but doesn't.

I go to Alessio and take his hand. "It's okay, Alessio."

"Anna, go outside. I need to speak to Alessio," Nikolai voices.

I can feel the tension in the room and despite knowing none of the men in this room would hurt me, I can't say the same about them hurting each other. I shake my head. "No whatever you want to speak about can be said in front of me."

Nikolai is glaring daggers into Alessio and vice versa. "Idi na ulitsu seychas." *Go outside now.*

"Carter, take Anna outside now," Alessio says to his brother without taking his eyes off Nikolai.

Carter steps forward and puts his hand on my arm and pulls me towards the door. I try to dig my heels but it's no use. Carter pulls me out like a ragdoll with little effort. I hear the door shut behind us.

I go to open it but find it's locked.

Alessio

When I went looking for Anna, I didn't expect to find her with her brothers. I know she misses her brothers, but I don't trust them one bit.

Nikolai's stance is casual, but his look is anything but. "I want my sister and her son back home."

"That's not happening." Anna is my wife and Daniele is my son. Over my dead body are they leaving.

"Name your price."

"She's not some piece of land or toy that can be bought," I argue.

Nikolai leans against his desk and crosses his legs at the ankles. "If my sister wants to leave and come home, you will not stop her." It's not a question but a statement.

"She is my wife, and he is my son. They are not going anywhere."

Maxim steps forward and Nico in response takes a step forward. We could all kill each other here in this room if we wanted to.

"They are not going anywhere," I repeat. "We're leaving." I turn and leave the office with Nico following behind me.

"What the fuck was that?" he hisses as soon as we are outside the office.

"No idea, but if they think they can take Anna or my son from me they are in for a surprise," I jeer back.

We exit the house and find Carter and Anna standing near our SUV. Anna is giving Carter a death glare while he shows indifference to my young wife's antics.

When she sees me, her face turns to relief. "What happened?"

I grab Anna's arm and pull her towards the SUV. "We are leaving."

"What?"

"Get in the car," I bark little too loudly, causing Anna to flinch and recoil. *Shit.* She hasn't reacted this way to me in months. I'm about to apologize when she turns around and gets in the SUV without saying a word.

My brothers give me a look, but I don't have time for this. "Let's go." I get in and Nico and Carter follow my lead.

We drive back in silence. We are getting near the penthouse when Anna turns in my direction. "What did you and my brothers talk about?"

"Nothing you have to worry about."

"I have a right to know."

"Your brother wants you back home."

Anna's eyes widen. "I can go back home." She says it like a revelation she just realized can leave.

"No, you can't." I enunciate each word.

"Why not?"

"You are not going anywhere!" I shout. She pulls back into her seat at my sudden outburst and turns away. I can see her fingers trembling in her lap.

We get to the penthouse and Anna gets out before anyone can even open her door and walks in. I follow behind her with Nico and Carter behind me.

Once in the elevator, I can feel the tension in the small composed space ready to explode. The elevators swing open to our floor and Anna walks out.

I'm about to step out when Nico grabs my shoulder. "Let's talk."

"About what?"

Nico hits the button for Carter's penthouse and the doors close shut. "What the hell was that about?"

I shrug not wanting to get into this with my brothers.

"You almost ripped her head off," Carter claims.

"I did not."

The elevator doors open to Carter's penthouse, and we step out.

Nico walks over to the bar at the side and begins making some drinks. "You did."

He makes two drinks and walks over to me. He hands one to me and the other to Carter and goes back to make himself another.

I drink it one big gulp. The alcohol burns my throat as it goes down. Nico grabs the bottle of alcohol and puts it down on the coffee table. I take a seat on the couch and pour another drink and drink that too in one go as well.

Nico takes a seat across from me. "Are you going to tell us why now?"

I slam the glass on the table in front of me. "She wants to leave."

Carter takes a seat next to Nico and leans back. "And you don't want her to?"

"She's my wife."

"She was forced into this marriage by Yuri. Now that he is dead, maybe she wants out."

The thought of Anna wanting out and leaving burns me more than the alcohol. "I don't understand why she wants to leave. I have tried my best to give her everything she wants."

Nico swirls his drink in his glass. "Sometimes people want more."

"What more could she want?"

"Someone who cares for them and is there for them. Love."

I take in Nico's words. I do care for Anna and have feelings for Anna but I don't know exactly what they are. I can't make sense of them, let alone explain them to someone else.

Nico seems to be lost in thought while staring into the liquid amber of his drink when he looks up. "If you want her to stay, you have to give her a reason, otherwise let her live her life. She deserves that at least after everything she has been through. No point in both you being stuck in a hopeless marriage."

Anna does deserve everything she wants. She was forced into this marriage by her father and then tortured by my enemies because of me. If she wants to leave, it should be her choice. "I need to talk to Anna." I get up from the couch and head towards the elevators.

CHAPTER 32

Anna

I'm furious at Alessio for how he reacted earlier.

He and my brothers had spoken and he decided I didn't get a say. It is my life they were discussing and I got no say in it.

I have lived my entire life with my papa deciding how I live my life and what I can or can't do. I won't allow Alessio to do the same. Especially when it has to do with the kids.

I need to put my foot down now or I won't get to make any decisions for my children's lives either. I want Emma and Daniele to be able to go out and live their life to the fullest. I don't want them to feel trapped or imprisoned.

Alessio might disagree with some of my decisions, but I want him to at least be open to discussing it. For us to make compromises and be partners rather than him deciding everything and me doing as he says.

I hear Daniele wail from the baby monitor and head towards his room. I get to his crib and rock him in my arms and lull him back to sleep.

As I'm rocking, I look around the room and realize even though I decorated the room, everything in here was picked out by someone and shipped to the penthouse. I didn't get to go out and pick out my son's bedroom décor.

After a few minutes of trying to get Daniele to sleep, I decide to feed him instead since he is up and feeding time will be soon.

I head towards the kitchen for the pumped milk I had put in the fridge earlier while I was at the funeral to warm it up.

Once the bottle is warmed up, I head back to the living room and take a seat on the couch and feed Daniele. He grabs at it with his small hands and begins sucking at it as soon as the tip touch's his small pink lips.

I run a finger over his soft brown hair. He opens his blue eyes that match mine and stares at me as he continues to drink.

The elevator rings open and I turn around to see Alessio walk in.

I'm still mad at him but having Daniele in my arms is thawing my anger every second.

Alessio comes around and takes a seat next to me. He uses the back of his index finger and runs it over Daniele's plump baby cheeks. "I'm sorry for yelling at you earlier."

I'm taken aback that Alessio is apologizing. Someone of his status and position doesn't usually apologize.

"It's okay," I say. Most of my anger has already evaporated thanks to Daniele and Alessio's apology melted whatever remained.

"If you want to go back home you can but Daniele stays."

My head snaps up towards Alessio so suddenly it makes Daniele squirm at my sudden shift in my arms. "What?!"

"If you want to leave, I won't hold you hostage, but my son stays with me." Alessio's voice is emotionless.

My anger is back in full blast. Ready to detonate in a fury. The fact that Alessio is telling me to abandon my son. "And Emma?" I grind out. I know the answer but I need to hear it.

"She is my daughter."

"And mine. Or did you suddenly decide I'm no longer Emma's mother? Is that how it's going to be? Whenever you feel like it, you throw it in my face that Emma is not my daughter." My voice rises with each word I spit out. My anger has reached a new level I didn't know was possible.

I push to my feet and start walking upstairs.

Alessio follows behind me. "You are Emma's mother. I didn't mean it like that. I just mean if you want to leave you can but my children stay here."

I whirl around on the steps of the stairs and face Alessio. Despite being two steps higher, I'm barely eye level to him but I don't let the height difference discourage me.

I look Alessio straight in the eyes. "Why would I leave my children?"

"Then what do you want?"

I spin back around and continue up the steps. Alessio continues to follow silently. Once I got to Daniele's room, I put him inside his crib gently. His eyes are closed, and he has fallen asleep despite mine and Alessio's argument.

I lean forward and kiss him on his forehead. When I turn around, I see Alessio standing at the doorway, watching. I make my way towards the door, but Alessio doesn't step aside. Instead, his muscled body is blocking my exit.

"Alessio," I whisper yell. I don't want to wake up Daniele, but my anger hasn't smothered. He takes a step to the side, and I exit.

When I get to my bedroom, I get the urge to slam it shut out of a tantrum, but I hold it in. Alessio isn't far behind, but I don't look back.

I head towards the closet and unzip out of my dress. I slide out of it and kick it to the side taking my frustration out on the poor fabric. I'm seeing red at this point, and I twirl around to go to the bathroom to shower when I walk straight into a hard body.

I take a step back and realize I walked right into Alessio's chest. I look up at him and see his eyes are an intense black. I'm confused by his reaction and how his eyes are fixated on me.

I look down at myself and realize I'm only wearing my black lace bra and lace panties.

Alessio's strong and powerful stare sends a throbbing heat between my body and the knot in my heart tightens further.

Alessio takes a step forward and the old part of me is telling me to run. But I hold my ground, I won't run and hide. At first, he is gentle. He lightly strokes my face and then traces a finger down my neck.

His fingers feel like it's leaving a scorching trail down my body. He leans forward and gently kisses me. I'm hesitant at first but relax at the feeling rising through my body. I'm filled with emotions and my head is clouded and I'm in a daze.

All of a sudden, he pulls me towards him and deepens the kiss. My body pressed into his and he backs me up until I hit the mattress and fall. Still in a daze, I let my emotions guide me for once then the fear.

Alessio undresses and is back on top of me. Seeing his naked body the knot gets tighter. Not telling me to stop or run but rather keep going. He is back on top of me kissing me and I kiss him back to the point of suffocation.

"Anna, tell me to stop and I will," he says breathlessly against my lips.

I know what he is saying but the feeling in my stomach is telling me to keep going. I grab my panties and push them down and kick them off. Alessio growls and positions himself between my legs.

Alessio parts my legs and kneels between them. Bracing himself on one muscled arm, he grabs his erection and runs the tip along my slit. I gasp at the firm pressure against my clit.

I'm getting closer, the knot deep inside of me trying to unravel. He brings his tip to my opening and pushes in a bit. I clench at the intrusion, even as my body begs for more. He pulls in and out. He pushes in deeper with every new thrust until finally, he fills me completely. Alessio's pelvis pressed up to mine, his hips parting me for him, his abs tensing, and the harsh lust on his gorgeous face blasted my knot finally to shreds.

I cry out as pleasure radiates through me with a force that makes me clench so tightly that Alessio exhales sharply from my pussy's grip on him. He slams harder into me as I sink my nails into his backside, lifting my hips almost frantically to meet his thrusts.

Alessio grips my hips in a bruising hold, jerking me faster against him until the slapping of our bodies and his grunts fills the room as he pounds into me. Soreness thrums through me, battling with the low hum of pleasure. I gasp and then moan.

His eyes burn into me as he breathes harshly. His moves become uncoordinated, his eyes wild. I hold onto his back desperately, overwhelmed by the sensations of pain and pleasure, by the feel of his heavy weight pressing me into the bed, by the scent of our mingled sweat and sex.

He thrusts harder, and then he tenses with a sharp exhale. I, too, freeze at the feeling of utter fullness, not sure if I was going to come apart at the seams. I feel his release deep inside of me and moan. This feels so good.

Alessio kisses me, then my throat, then pants. "You are mine. There is no leaving now." He presses a kiss to my temple then rolls off me and onto his back while pulling me towards him.

I try to catch my breath and make sense of his words but I'm too exhausted and I fall asleep.

Alessio

Anna is asleep on top of me after I pulled her into my hold. I can feel her breath on my chest as she breathes in and out.

When I told her earlier she could leave, I wanted her to be happy. I didn't want to hold on to her and imprison her like her father. I wanted her to have a choice. I didn't mean I would keep the kids away from her. I would never do that to them or her. Emma loves Anna and she would be heartbroken if she left.

However, the safest place for my children is beside me. I don't trust Nikolai or the Petrovs to keep my children protected.

As I was telling Anna she could go back home, despite keeping my voice unwavering, it felt as though my heart was being split open. I didn't want her to go and now I don't think I can.

I push back Anna's soft silky blonde hair away from her face and kiss the top of her head.

I gave Anna a choice earlier but now I'm not giving her that choice anymore. I will do whatever it takes to keep her beside me.

CHAPTER 33

Anna

Alessio has finally agreed to let us out. With my papa dead and the only threat being Ronan, he thinks it's safe to go out as long as we are with a number of guards. Or as safe as it can be considering your husband is the Italian mafia boss.

During breakfast when Alessio announced I am no longer on house arrest, I actually jumped out of my seat out of excitement. I'm not sure if it was his way of apologizing for what he said yesterday but I'm still angry and being allowed out isn't going to make me forgive him that easily. His words were hurtful, and I won't be pushed around anymore.

Having sex may have not been the smartest thing at the moment but I have no regrets. It may have actually helped in my healing process. A part of me still feared Alessio and the physical component of our relationship but now I feel like a wall that was put in place has been broken down.

Emma and I are walking down the street to a coffee shop near the penthouse. I didn't bring Daniele with us since it's freezing cold, and I didn't want him to catch a cold. He is only a few weeks old.

The streets are filled with lights and Christmas decorations. Everyone is buzzing by us with full shopping bags. Christmas eve is tomorrow, and I still don't know what to get Alessio.

I bought toys and clothes for Emma and Daniele and even found something for Nico, Carter, Greta and even Gia.

Gia still hasn't come to see Daniele. Every interaction with her has been awful but I thought I would try and make peace with her. We are family and are stuck together.

Alessio has decided to throw a last-minute Christmas party considering all the events and parties we have missed this year due to everything that has happened the last several months. He wants to show everyone we are not hiding and are in control.

When he told me I almost blew a gasket at the thought of the preparations needed to be done. But he assured me everything will be taken care of and I had nothing to worry about but to show up.

I check my phone for any messages. My brothers have not contacted me since the funeral. I know they want me back home, but I can't leave my children. Despite being forced into this marriage with Alessio, we have made it work for the most part. It may not be the most conventional marriage but it's working.

We get to the coffee shop and I open the door for Emma to walk in first. The heat hits you as soon as you walk in.

I grab Emma's hand to keep sight of her in the rush of people in the coffee shop and get in line. Our new guard Dino is standing near the door. I had wanted him to keep a distance but considering Ronan and other threats out there I asked him to try and blend in instead. His large body and figure makes it hard but I can tell he is trying.

"Dino, what would you like?"

"Nothing, ma'am." I frown at him calling me ma'am, I've asked him numerous times to call me Anna, but he insists on keeping things formal.

Emma tugs on my arm, "I want hot cocoa, Mommy."

"Okay, my love."

We get to the front of the line and I order three hot chocolates. One for Dino even though he said no. I plan on winning him over slowly and hopefully getting him to drop the ma'am.

I grab the first hot chocolate and turn around and hand one to Dino who takes it with a big smile. Despite his giant size, he reminds me of a cuddly bear. That is when he smiles. When he is all business, he looks more like a grizzly bear ready to shred you into pieces.

I grab the last two and start walking towards an empty table. Emma tugs on my arm to grab the hot chocolate but it's still too hot for her. "Go sit down, my love." I tip my chin towards the empty chair and Emma climbs onto the chair.

I take the one across it and see that Dino has moved to the corner to keep an eye from a distance while having a visual of the entire shop.

I pop off the lid of the hot chocolate and blow on it a few times. Emma's eyes are like two large saucers watching me. I smile and hand the now cooled-down hot chocolate to her and she grabs it instantly.

"Your daughter is beautiful, just like her mother." I look up and see a dark-haired man standing near our table.

"Oh, thank you."

He walks over to our table and grabs a chair from the table beside us and pulls it to ours and takes a seat. "I hope you don't mind it's a bit crowded here." It is crowded in here but the table he pulled the chair from was empty and he could have taken the seat there.

"I'm Peter." He holds out his hand.

Unsure what to do, I shake his hand. "Hi, I'm Anna."

"What is someone as beautiful as you doing out and about in the cold?"

"My daughter and I decided to do some last-minute Christmas shopping and stopped by for something warm."

"Is that so? Well, you're in luck because I know some great shops to buy presents from."

"I think we are okay, thank you." I hope he gets the hint and leaves.

He grabs my hand. "I won't take no for an answer."

I try to pull away, but he holds my hand captive. I'm about to turn around and signal for Dino to come when I see a shadow fall over us. I look up thinking it's Dino but instead find it's Alessio. His face is filled with rage. "Hands off my wife."

Peter cranes his neck up to Alessio and his eyes widen in fear. He instantly lets go of my hand and stumbles to his feet. "Sorry, I didn't know she was married." Peter slides away almost like a snake slithering away and heads straight for the exit as if the building is on fire.

Alessio narrows his eyes on me. "What were you doing?"

"Nothing."

"Nothing?" he repeats.

I don't understand why he is asking me. I didn't do anything wrong. Peter was the one who initiated the conversation, took a seat, and grabbed my hand. Plus, I'm still mad at him.

Emma finishes her hot chocolate and pushes the cup away. "All done."

"That's my girl." I grab her hand and kiss it, making her giggle. "Let's go shopping now." We get up from our seats and start walking out with Alessio following behind. Once outside I turn to Alessio. "I guess we will see you at home."

"So, you can do *nothing* with more guys," Alessio scoffs.

"I did *nothing*. He came up to me. What was I supposed to do, tell him to go away?"

Alessio gives me a chilling smile. "Either you tell him to go away or," he leans forward into my ear, "I shoot them dead."

I face Alessio in shock, our noses almost touching. "You wouldn't."

Alessio straightens to his full height. "I would if they touch what's mine."

"I'm not yours," I counter.

Alessio drops his smile and his eyes storm with an unrecognizable emotion.

Emma tugs on my jacket sleeve. "Mommy, let's go." I grab her small hand into mine and start walking. I can hear Alessio's footsteps behind us. After a few minutes of walking, I stop and turn around. "Don't you have work?"

"Nope. In fact, I have to grab some things too."

I don't buy his lie but let it go.

We pass by a ballet shop and Emma peers up at the outfits hanging in the window. "Wow, is that a princess outfit?" she asks in awe.

"No, my love, that is a ballet outfit for ballerinas."

"I want to do ballet."

I crouched down to her level. "You do?"

Emma nods in excitement. "The princess in the nutcracker does ballet."

I recall Emma watching the Nutcracker ballet a few days ago with me and how she mimicked the dance. I didn't think anything of it, but this could be a good chance for Emma to try a new hobby.

I stand and face Alessio. "I think we should put Emma in ballet."

"She's too young for it."

"I started ballet when I was three."

"You did ballet?" Alessio voices with surprise.

"Yes, for a few years. My mother was a ballerina and I wanted to follow in her footsteps."

"Why did you stop?"

I try to keep my voice smooth to prevent my emotions from seeping through. "My papa said it reminded him of my mother and made me stop." He hated my mother for killing herself. He called her weak and pathetic, but I now know she must have been in tremendous pain to take her own life.

Alessio doesn't say a word, but I can feel him assessing me, trying to get into my head. Alessio nods. "Okay."

Emma jumps up in excitement next to me. "Mommy, I'm going to be a princess."

I pick Emma up into my arms and give her a kiss on the cheek. "My love, you already are one." I walk into the ballet shop and decide to buy Emma her first ballet outfit.

CHAPTER 34

Anna

I t's Christmas eve and the penthouse is decorated like a Christmas book catalog.

I walk into Emma's room and see her pouting in the corner with her dollhouse. She wanted to attend the party, but she is too young to attend right now. Instead, Greta will watch Emma and Daniele upstairs as the party takes place downstairs.

Emma looks up from her toy dolls and her eyes widen. "Mommy, you look like a princess."

I smile. "Thank you, my love," I say and give her a kiss on her crown.

I opted for a red off-the-shoulder gown that hugs my curves. Since having Daniele my boobs have grown in size and the top emphasizes it in a classy way. My hair is done in loose waves and my makeup is kept natural.

"I need you to stay up here with Greta and be a good girl," I say to Emma.

She pouts. "Okay." Her voice barely above a whisper.

I smooth down her fluffy brown hair. "I have a surprise for you. When you wake up tomorrow morning on Christmas day, it will be waiting."

Emma's eyes shine. "Promise?"

"Promise." I give her another kiss and head downstairs to see how the setup is going.

Once downstairs, I check on the caterers who assure me everything is on schedule, and I have nothing to worry about. Despite everyone's constant confirmations, I can't help but feel anxious.

As the wife of the Capo, all eyes are going to be on me. Despite everyone smiling and putting up a front of kindness, behind those exteriors are vultures waiting for me to mess up.

I head back towards the living room and find Alessio chatting away with his brothers.

He is dressed in a black suit with a black tie and looks absolutely handsome.

Alessio turns and meets my eyes. His intense gaze makes me feel as though the entire room lacks oxygen. I've never felt this way before about anyone. I've always been too busy being wary of their intentions to take the time to actually see them as a person.

Alessio has not only gained my trust but is slowly making me fall for him. I'm not someone who lets anyone in easily, but he has broken down each of my walls and yet makes me feel safe.

Alessio says something to his brothers and walks over to me. He leans forward and gives me a light kiss on the cheek. "You look beautiful." So light yet sends a scorching heat down my body.

I gave him a small smile and just as I'm about to tell him he looks amazing as well, I'm interrupted by the elevator chime.

The guests start to pour in, and we make our way to greet the guests. Each guest is polite and full of compliments. Some seem genuine, others not so much but hope to gain favor with Alessio.

Gia walks in with her very bright pink gown. She looks even more unrecognizable than the last time I saw her. I'm assuming she got some more work done or at least had some botox injected.

"Alessio, what a lovely party," she hums in annoyance. She glances from the corner of her eye at me but doesn't bother to look my way or acknowledge me. "I know how much Maria loved Christmas and this was her favorite time." Gia smirks. "I'm sure she would have loved this."

I go rigid at the mention of Maria. I have asked Greta a few questions about Maria but no one else has dared bring up Maria in my presence.

I have nothing against her but considering she was Alessio's first wife and Emma's mother, it does make me uncomfortable having Gia speak about her. Maria is also a reminder that Alessio and Emma are not really mine. I am just a replacement.

"I should check on the caterers," I excuse myself and make my way to the kitchen, needing the space.

Once in the kitchen, the staff is buzzing around getting dishes ready and putting them on trays. I'm clearly in their way so I head back out only to run into Alessio in the hallway.

"Are you okay?" His brown eyes are soft with concern. He is always concerned about me and looking out for me. Besides my brothers, no one has really done that. Even my own papa didn't care how I felt.

"I'm okay. We should get back to our guests."

"You shouldn't listen to Gia. She's a spiteful and miserable person."

"I know." I want to ask Alessio about Maria but now is not the time with dozens of guests waiting for us.

I try to walk past Alessio, but he grabs my shoulders and cages me in place. His gaze roams over my face as if trying to find something out of place. He drops his hands. "Okay, let's get back to the guests."

I nod and we head back out.

Alessio

Stupid Gia had to say something rude and inconsiderate again. She brought Maria up knowing it would hurt Anna. She said she was okay, but I can see the hurt in her eyes. She was never good at hiding her emotions.

Anna is across the room chatting up with some of the wives of other underbosses and captains. Most of them are a lot older but I can see they adore Anna. Despite her young age, she is intelligent, generous, and gracious. It is hard not to like her.

In her red gown, she looks stunningly gorgeous. I can't help but watch her from the other side of the room.

Nico comes to stand beside me. "I heard about Gia being Gia. Sorry." He shakes his head. "I don't know what I can do about her."

It's not Nico's fault Gia behaves the way she does. But I have allowed her to get away with too much. I gave her a pass for many years because she was Maria's best friend and Nico's wife. She is part of the family, but I've had it. She's rude and obnoxious to Anna and I won't have anyone disrespect or hurt her.

"This is the last time she will be allowed at any family event. From now on she is banned from all events and parties. I won't have her upsetting Anna again."

Nico looks surprised. "I don't have a problem with that. I've wanted her out for years. I just didn't think you would agree. Considering she is my wife and her being banned would not look good."

"I don't care how it looks anymore," I snap.

Nico laughs. Actually, laughs at this moment. "I knew you had feelings for Anna, but I didn't know it was this bad."

"What does that supposed to mean?"

Nico slaps my back and continues to laugh. "You are so fucked."

CHAPTER 35

Anna

The party was amazing, and everything went as planned. I say goodbye to the last guests and make my way back to the living room.

Nico and Carter are about to head out when I stop them. I grab the presents I got for them from under the tree and hand them over. They both look surprised I got them anything.

"If I had known, I would have gotten something for you," Nico says.

I wave a hand in the air. "No, you don't have to get me anything. Besides, you might not even like it."

Nico smiles. "I doubt that. Anything from you we would love." Nico can be very charming. I had heard some of the ladies even call him prince charming.

"Oh wait," I head back to the tree and grab another present, "this one is for Gia." I hand it to Nico who is hesitant to take it.

Gia had left before I could give it to her personally but she also spent most of the night ignoring me or on the other end of the room as if I was a contagious deadly virus.

Alessio comes to stand beside me. "Why did you get her anything?"

"She's family."

Alessio furrows his brows in confusion.

"I'm sure she will love it too," Nico says with confidence. One would believe it if I didn't know Gia. She will probably hate it but it's an olive branch. One I am hoping she accepts.

Nico and Carter both give me a hug and thank me for their gifts and head out.

Alessio wraps a hand around my waist and pulls me towards him. I shudder at his sudden touch and closeness. "That was nice of you. Despite how Gia treated you, you included her."

I try and lean back but Alessio has me pinned to his body. "Like I said, she's family."

He smiles. "I got you something too."

"You did!" I shriek unladylike. But I'm too excited at Alessio getting me a gift.

I haven't gotten any gifts in a while. A few times my brothers would get me something for Christmas or my birthday when I was younger but when Papa found out he threw them in the trash, stating I didn't deserve it. After that, it was better not to receive anything than to get something and have it taken away.

In the last couple of years, the only real gift I received was the snowflake bracelet my brother Damien got me before he died. To me, it wasn't a gift but a reminder of my brother.

Alessio chuckles at my excitement and I can feel his body vibrate with laughter. He lets me go and walks over to the Christmas tree. "Close your eyes and stick out your hands."

I hesitate at first thinking this might be a trick. But Alessio isn't my papa. He wouldn't hurt me.

I close my eyes and put my hands out in front of me. I feel something land in my hand. I open my eyes and see it's a small box wrapped in gold paper with a red bow at the top.

I take a seat on the couch and put the box in my lap and just stare at it. My first real present that can't be taken away.

"Are you going to open it?" Alessio asks.

"No."

"No?" Alessio looks at me as if I'm a complicated puzzle.

I feel the gold gift wrap paper and can't help the emotions that arise through me.

Alessio sighs and takes a seat next to me. "You haven't even opened it and you already don't like it."

I turn towards him. "No, I love it!"

Alessio looks at me as though he doesn't believe me.

"I really do love it," I say. "It's just my first real gift in a long time."

Alessio is stunned. "You never received a gift before?"

"I've received this from my brother." I shake the bracelet on my wrist. "But besides that, no, not in a while. Any time I did receive anything when I was younger, my papa would take it away."

Something dark passes over Alessio's face. "Your father died too easily."

I laugh. "I doubt that. My brothers wouldn't have given papa an easy death." They hated Papa more than I did.

Knowing my brothers, they most likely killed Papa in the most painful way possible and stretched it out to last. After all that he has done, he wouldn't get an easy way out.

"So," Alessio tilts his head and smirks, "are you not going to open it? If I knew a simple box would make you happy, I would have saved my money."

As much as I would love to keep it as is, I'm curious as to what Alessio got me. I gently remove the bow and unwrap the paper.

It's a black velvet box. I open the small box and inside are two snowflake diamond earrings, matching to my bracelet. "It's beautiful." My breath is taken away.

"I'm glad you like it."

"I love it." Without thinking I wrap my arms around Alessio and hug him. He gives me a kiss on the top of the head making me melt at his touch.

I look up at him and I can't help but push up and kiss him. His lips feel warm against mine and I can feel a tingling sensation rising between my legs.

I pull Alessio closer to me and he moans against my lips. "Anna, we need to stop."

"Why?" As much as I feared being near Alessio before, I have now grown comfortable with him. Maybe a little too comfortable.

"Because Greta is upstairs, and the caterers are still here cleaning up."

I pull away realizing we are not alone, and I was just about to jump Alessio out in the open.

Alessio chuckles. "We can finish this later." He gives me a peck on the lips before he pulls away and heads to the kitchen to check on the caterers.

Slowly Alessio is melting away all the pain I've kept hidden inside for so long.

CHAPTER 36

Alessio

I t's early morning on Christmas day and still dark outside. After the carters and Greta left for the night, I found Anna upstairs putting on the snowflake earrings.

Despite us having sex the night before, I had worried it may have been a one time thing due to rising emotions in the moment.

But in the living room, I could tell she wanted more. It took all my will power to wait until the penthouse was empty.

I've held off for months while Anna was pregnant and used all my pent-up frustration to take it out on the Irish.

With Maria, I could have had someone on the side, and she wouldn't have cared as long as she didn't have to hear about it.

But since getting married to Anna, my mind is constantly filled with thoughts of her. I don't want anyone else but her.

Thankfully when I got to the bedroom and grabbed her by the waist, she melted into my touch and was ready for more.

I probably should have gone slow but like last time I couldn't hold it in. I needed her right then and there. I pulled her towards me and ripped her dress trying to get her out of it. I regret it now because she looked amazing in that dress.

Her naked body is now pressed against me. She fell asleep after the second round. I could have gone for a third, but I could tell

Anna was sore. She just had Daniele a few weeks ago and hasn't fully healed. I need to go slower with her next time.

I hear the door creak and on instinct, I go to grab my gun from the bedside table drawer.

I switch the light on ready to shoot when I realize the intruder is none other than my precious daughter.

Her brown hair is a mess, and her eyes are half shut. I click on the safety of the gun and hide it under my pillow.

"Mia Cara, what are you doing here?"

"It's Christmas day, Daddy." She trudges over to me and tries to climb into bed.

I put my hands under her armpits and pick her up. "It's early. Go to sleep."

Emma pouts. "No it's Christmas, and Mommy promised me a present if I was good. I was good."

I smile at Emma and give her a kiss on the cheek. "I know you have been good."

Emma leans over and tries to shake Anna awake beside me. Anna peels her eyes open and turns to me. In a hoarse sleep voice, she asks "What time is it?"

"Five am."

Anna groans at the mention of the time.

Emma shakes Anna again with her little hands. "Mommy, you promised."

I'm just about to tell Emma enough is enough when Anna rolls to the side of the bed. She grabs my discarded shirt from the ground and while gripping the bedsheet to herself and puts it on.

She stretches out her arms above her head once she has buttoned up the shirt. "Okay, my love, I'm up."

Emma wiggles out of my grasp and jumps across the bed into Anna's arms. Anna smiles and gives Emma a kiss on the forehead. "Let's go see what Santa brought you."

Anna and Emma head downstairs and I'm left speechless in bed. The patience and love Anna has surprises me each day.

I kick the blanket off and put on a pair of sweatpants and follow them downstairs.

As I'm nearing the bottom of the steps, I hear Emma scream, "Wow!" By the time I've reached the living room, Emma has dived into the pile of presents under the tree.

Anna is awake on the couch in nothing but my shirt watching Emma. She looks breathtakingly beautiful. When she sees me, she gets up. "I'm going to check on Daniele. Can you watch her and make sure she doesn't topple the tree down trying to open gifts?"

"Of course." As Anna walks by, I grab her around the waist and pull her towards me and give her a kiss. She looks stunned at first but then gives me a warm smile as she pulls away. I release her and she walks back upstairs.

Emma has found a large wrapped box and is struggling trying to pull it out. I walk towards her and give her a hand.

I help her unwrap her presents and with each gift she opens she gets more excited.

Not all of them are toys. Some of the presents I noticed Anna bought were practical things like winter boots and jackets.

In a span of ten minutes, the living room looks as though it has been hit by a tornado sending wrapping paper and gifts in every direction.

Anna comes down with a now awake Daniele in her arms and she takes a seat on the couch next to me. "I see she has opened almost all of her gifts."

"She has."

Emma turns to Anna. "Mommy, can I open Daniele's gifts too?"

"Daniele is too little to open gifts so he could use the help. As his big sister, I think he would like it if you helped."

Emma gives a full-face grin. "Okay!" And so, begins round two of opening gifts.

After a few minutes, Emma crawls under the tree and finds a small box wrapped up. "What's this?" She looks at it confused.

"Let me see," I ask. Emma hands me the box and I see there's no name on it.

"Oh right, that is the present I got for Emma," Anna recalls.

I hand the wrapped box to Emma, who opens it in a hurry, ripping the gift wrap into shreds and tossing it to the side. It's a small rectangle white box. Emma hands it to me. "Daddy, open it."

I open the white box to a gold bracelet with little snowflakes like Anna's.

"It's like Mommy's." Emma beams.

"It is. My brother gave me mine so he can find me if I ever get lost," Anna says to Emma. "With this, if you ever get lost, me and Daddy will find you."

Anna got Emma the same bracelet in case she ever gets kidnapped again.

"Daddy, put it on me." Emma sticks out her hand for me to put on her bracelet.

I take out the bracelet from the box and put it on my small innocent daughter's petite wrist. She smiles as she shakes the bracelet on her wrist.

A lump forms in my throat and I swallow it down at the thought that Emma may get taken again. Anna must have had the same thought and decided to take measures in case that ever happens. But I will never let anyone hurt my family again.

CHAPTER 37

Anna

I t's eight am and I made basic pancakes for breakfast.

Greta has the day off for Christmas and since I've been up since five am, I wasn't in the mood to make a grand breakfast.

Thankfully Alessio and Emma didn't complain. I just put Daniele in his crib for his nap when my phone rings.

It's a text from an unknown number. I open the text and I know it's from my brother Nikolai. He used the secret code numbers at the end of the texts. We formed secret codes to warn one another when Papa was angry or was up to no good.

He is asking me to meet him around the block at the park. I message back saying I will meet him in fifteen minutes.

I quickly change into a sweater, skinny jeans, knee-high boots and top it off with a jacket.

I get downstairs and find Alessio is on his phone while watching Emma play with her new toys in the living room. When he looks up and sees me, he gets up instantly. "Where are you going?"

"My brother Nikolai messaged me and wants to meet me at the park." I tell him the truth. Things have been good with me and Alessio and I don't want to lie.

"No." His voice is firm. Alessio crosses his arms against his chest. "It's not safe. Besides, Dino is off today."

"He is my brother. He would never hurt me." I know Alessio doesn't trust my brothers. Considering Papa had backstabbed him, I'm not surprised. But I know my brother's inside and out. Alessio doesn't.

Alessio shakes his head. "No."

Alessio rarely says no to me but I'm not taking no for an answer. He can't stop me from seeing my brother. I move towards the elevator and hit the button to call it up.

"Anna," Alessio warns.

The elevator swings open and I enter.

Alessio jumps over the couch and charges towards the elevator like a panther targeting his prey.

I quickly hit the ground floor button numerous times to shut the doors. The doors slam shut just as Alessio is nearing, missing him by a millisecond.

I breathe out a sigh of relief and slump against the wall. That was close.

The elevator gets to the ground floor and I make my way outside. I make the five-minute walk to the park and look around for Nikolai. It's freezing cold.

I should have worn a scarf and gloves, but I was in such a rush to get here I didn't think about my outfit.

I see Nikolai at the other end of the park and I walk towards him. He is wearing a black suit, jacket, and leather gloves. When I am at a reaching distance from him, I run to him and give him a hug.

He hugs me back. "Anna, we need to talk."

I pull away from my brother. "About what?"

"I'm planning on getting you out of your marriage from Alessio. You can come back home."

"I can't come home. I can't leave my children."

Nikolai gives me a knowing look. "I know. That is why I'm going to take care of Alessio."

"Take care?" I falter. "What do you mean by that?"

"The less you know the better."

"No." I shake my head. "You can't hurt Alessio."

"Anna."

"He is my husband. And…" I trail off. I almost confessed I care and have feelings for Alessio, but the truth is I'm not sure what my feelings are yet.

Nikolai puts his hand on my shoulder. "Anna, I need you to tell me now. If you want out, I can get you out."

"I don't want out," I pause. "What I want is for you and Alessio to be okay with one another. I know neither of you trust one another but I want you both in my life. I want all my brothers in my life. My life with Alessio and my children." The thought of having to choose between my brothers and my family with Alessio is heart-wrenching.

Nikolai drops his hand from my shoulder and nods. "Okay."

"Okay?"

He gives me a smile. "Yeah, okay. I will sort things out with Alessio."

"And by sort you mean?" I push for more information.

"Not kill. But call a truce and renegotiate an alliance that will keep you safe and give you what you want. But if you ever want out in the future, I need you to tell me."

I smile and hug my big brother. He always looked out for me and took care of me since I was a baby. "Thank you."

Alessio

I'm furious at Anna. How could she be so careless? I know Nikolai is her brother, but she is trusting too much. She doesn't know the dark side of him like I do.

The stories I've heard are unsettling, to say the least. It could be a trap to kidnap her or worse he could kill her.

I get a text from Nico advising Anna is on her way back. When Anna left unprotected, I called Nico and filled him in. He followed her to the park to make sure she stayed safe. I would have gone myself, but I had Emma and Daniele. Not to mention I would have dragged her back kicking and screaming.

I try to calm myself, but the anger is at its tipping point. I wouldn't hurt a hair on Anna's head but in my state, I know I would scare her the very least.

A few minutes later the elevator doors slide open and Anna walks in. My attempt to squash my anger is trampled as soon as I see her.

I march towards her in large steps. Anna's eyes widen and she tries to back away but I'm quicker. I reach for her and pull her towards me, throwing her over my shoulder.

Emma looks up from her game. "What's going on, Daddy?"

I turn around. "Nothing, just keep playing. Mommy and I will be right back." Anna tries to squirm out of my hold but I tighten my grasp on her and head towards my office.

Once I'm in my office, I slam the door shut with my foot and walk over to the couch in the corner and throw Anna on it.

She is frozen on the spot, unsure what to do.

I begin to pace back and forth trying to form my thoughts without going off on her.

"What were you thinking? You could have gotten hurt or kidnapped. He might be your brother, but you don't know what he is thinking or capable of. Not to mention you left the building without security. What if someone grabbed you while you were on your way to meet your brother? Ronan is still out there. You didn't even think of the risks or dangers you would be in. How about Emma and Daniele? Did you think what would happen to them if something happened to you? You are no longer allowed to leave the penthouse without my approval!" My attempt to keep calm is thrown out the window with each sentence I speak.

Anna gets up from the couch. "Without your approval? That's not happening. I have lived by my papa's rules from the day I was born. I will not live by your rules as well. I didn't think of the dangers I would be in, but I trust my brother. You say I don't know him, but I know him better than most people including you. If I want to see him or any of my brothers, you can't stop me!" Anna stomps towards the door in anger.

As she tries to open the door, I slam it shut. Her body flinches and I know I'm scaring her, but I need her to know she can't just do whatever she wants. I have given her whatever she wants out of fear of losing her, but I won't jeopardize her safety.

I lean forward towards her. "You will listen to what I say."

Anna spins around and I can see the tremor in her hand, but she is not backing down. "No."

"Anna!"

Her eyes fill with tears. "I will not be a prisoner here too. I can't. Not again." A tear drops down her cheek.

I sigh and press my forehead against the door above her. I don't want her to feel like a prisoner.

I straighten. "You are not a prisoner. You will never be a prisoner. But I can't have you running out into a dangerous situation."

"You wouldn't let me see Nikolai," she croaks as more tears fall down her perfect porcelain skin.

"I was worried about you."

She looks up at me with those beautiful ocean blue eyes and shakes her head. "I don't know how to make this work."

I step back. "What do you mean?"

"This marriage. I don't know how to make this work." Anna turns her back to me and opens the door and leaves.

CHAPTER 38

Alessio

Anna has kept her distance for the rest of the day. I don't know what she meant when she said she doesn't know how to make this marriage work, but I plan on talking to her.

I exploded at her in anger. I don't want to lose her because of what I said. I can't lose her.

I find her sitting on the couch in the living room. Both the children are asleep and now it's just the two of us. I won't let her run this time.

I stand above her, and she peers up from the book she is reading. She sighs and closes her book. "Alessio, we need to talk."

"I know." I walk over to the alcohol cabinet and make myself a drink. "I'm sorry I exploded at you earlier. I was worried when you left without protection."

Anna gets up from the couch and walks over to me and leans against the table I'm making my drink on. "I understand why you were worried. You don't trust my brother. And it was foolish of me to leave without protection. But I won't be told what to do. Not anymore."

I take a sip of my drink and face my wife. My beautiful wife who fought for our children. Who loves openly and despite my shortcomings stood by me.

I tuck a piece of hair behind her ear, and she shudders at my touch. "I don't want you to leave."

She cocks her head to the side. "You don't?"

"No."

"Last time you said I could leave," she points out.

I shake my head. "I changed my mind."

"You changed your mind?" she repeats what I said.

I finish my drink and grab Anna's hand and pull her towards a chair next to the alcohol cabinet. I take a seat and wrap my arm around her waist and pull her into my lap.

She tries to get up, but I hold her in place. She looks at me with confusion and uncertainty.

"I don't know what's between us, but I know I have feelings for you. When I married you, I thought you would just be someone to take care of Emma. I didn't expect myself to form an attachment to you. If I get angry at you, it's because I care. I am not trying to imprison you. I am concerned about you. And no matter how angry I get, I will never hurt you. I need you to know that."

Anna freezes on my lap. "You have feelings for me?" Her cheeks go pink.

Sometimes I forget how old she is. Anna is mature for her age and, after everything she's been through, strong too.

I smirk at her reaction. "Yes, I do."

"What about Maria?" Anna asks hesitantly. "She was your first wife; what was your relationship like with her?"

I knew we would have this conversation one day. "Maria was my wife and my friend. I knew her before I got married and stayed friends after."

Anna's brows furrow. "Did you love her?"

"As a friend." I tell her the truth. Maria and I never had the type of connection me and Anna have.

I'm not sure if I love Anna but I know it's stronger than what I had with Maria.

Despite being husband and wife, Maria and I lived two separate lives. She had her life with Gia and I had one with my brothers.

We barely interacted aside from having small conversations to keep in touch. I cared for Maria but only as a friend.

When she was killed it crushed me. I was supposed to protect her, and I had failed her. I slaughtered those responsible for her death in a form of redemption for my failure.

Anna nods knowingly. "Truth is I have feelings for you too. I don't know what they are exactly, but I know I can't leave either."

"You won't leave me." I smile at her acknowledgment of her feelings for me but more that she will stay.

She shakes her head. "No."

I feel up her soft leg and she quivers at my touch. I kiss her and pull her towards me. She moans against my mouth.

"Let's go to bed."

CHAPTER 39

Anna

The last couple of days have been amazing. Alessio and I are on the same page. We both have feelings for one another and despite not knowing what they are, I know it's strong.

It's New Year's Eve and I'm meeting Alessio at one of the bars, called The Taste Lounge, that the Vitale Family owns.

I opted for a strapless navy mini dress with gold strappy heels. I have my hair up in a loose messy hair bun and I'm wearing the gold diamond snowflake earrings Alessio gave me for Christmas.

Greta is watching Emma and Daniele and will be staying the night in the guest bedroom allowing us to stay out late. Not sure how late considering I'm usually exhausted by 10 pm these days.

I walk into The Taste Lounge, and it's decorated with gold and silver balloons and streamers. It's an upscale bar with dark authentic wood flooring to give a warm feel. I don't see Alessio, but I see some wives I have met at previous parties and decide to make my rounds and say hello.

Each one compliments on how beautiful I look and how I've lost my pregnancy weight so quickly.

I want to roll my eyes at some of them as they are trying way too hard with the compliments but smile and nod instead.

One of the wives is going on about how she wished she could go to Aspen for winter but had to stay in the city because of the Ronan debacle. It's not like she and her daughter were kidnapped or tortured, yet the way she speaks you would think the world has ended.

Feeling myself getting annoyed at the conversation, I excuse myself and grab a glass of white wine from the bar. I pumped milk for Daniele before I left so I can fully enjoy tonight.

It's the first night I get to go out and have fun on New Year's.

I grab my wine glass and see Nico sitting in the corner with another man at a table. I decide to make my way towards them and greet them.

When I near the table the other man at the table sees me and gets up from his chair to greet me. After a short greeting, he quickly excuses himself leaving me and Nico alone.

I slide into the seat across from him. "I don't see Gia. Is she coming later?"

Nico smiles. "Nope. She has been banned by Alessio after how she treated you."

I'm shocked that Alessio banned Gia. "I'll talk to Alessio." I don't want there to be any problems within the family because of me.

Nico shakes his head. "No, don't. She deserves it. Plus, I don't have to deal with her nagging at me throughout the night."

"You and Gia don't seem to like each other much."

Nico laughs. "Isn't it obvious?"

"Why did you marry her?"

"Gia had told me she was pregnant." Nico swallows his drink and slams it on the table. "Turns out it was a lie."

"I'm sorry." I don't know what else to say. I assumed Nico and Gia married for political reasons or were arranged between families like me and Alessio. To think Gia tricked Nico into marriage is horrible. They can't even divorce since they are Catholic.

"Did she like the gift I got her for Christmas?" I try to change the topic.

"Yeah, she loved it," Nico says firmly. One would believe such a lie, but I know better.

I smile sadly. "She hated it, didn't she?" I wanted her to like it and hopefully see it as an opportunity for us to at least be civil. Neither one of us is going anywhere.

Nico rubs the back of his neck in surprise. "Shit, usually I'm a better liar than that."

"It's okay. Where is Alessio? I don't see Carter either." I again change the topic to prevent things from getting awkward.

"Carter is dealing with some work. Alessio should be arriving any moment now."

As if on cue, Alessio walks into the bar, looking dashing as ever. He searches the room and once our eyes meet, he walks towards our table.

I rise as he reaches the table, and he puts his arm around my waist and gives me a kiss on the top of my head.

Nico gets up from the table. "I need a drink" he says and heads towards the bar.

I turn to Alessio. "I heard you banned Gia. You didn't have to do that. I want you to unban her."

Alessio shakes his head. "No, she needs to learn her place. In a few months, I might reconsider but for now, she is banned."

I give up trying to argue. I know Alessio won't bend. When he's made his decision, he sticks by it. And I have no plans to ruin my night by fighting with Alessio for Gia.

Alessio

Despite it being New Year's Eve, most of the night is spent reassuring the other underbosses that the Russians are not a threat and the Irish will be dealt with.

Nico has taken it upon himself to deal with Ronan. He has spent several weeks running leads on where Ronan is. Last we heard he was in Chicago making a deal with the Mancini family. Since then, no word on what was decided between the two or where he is now.

The Russians on the other hand have not made a move since Nikolai has taken over.

We have no reason to fight but considering Nikolai wanted Anna back home, I still consider him a threat.

When I had asked Anna about her meeting with her brother, she stated it was nothing but a siblings' meeting. She was very vague on what was discussed but she is certain it was nothing to worry about.

I may not trust Nikolai, but I know Anna wouldn't betray me. She had plenty of opportunities but instead stuck by me.

Anna looks gorgeous as always tonight in her tight navy dress. I've caught a few men staring but as soon as they made eye contact with me, they diverted their gaze.

It's almost near midnight and I head towards Anna. The women she is speaking to quickly scurry when they see me coming.

She turns around in confusion and her face softens when she sees me. I grab her small hand into mine and pull her towards an empty table. I take a seat and she wraps her arm around my neck and sits on my lap.

Her cheeks are flushed and her eyes are glazed. She's had a couple of drinks but not to the point she is sloppy.

"We should go out more often." Anna grins with happiness. I can tell she loves going out. She hasn't confirmed it but from what I previously heard, her father had kept her locked away. I don't ever plan on doing the same. I like seeing Anna happy.

"We don't have any upcoming events or parties anytime soon with the holidays over."

Anna purses her lips. "So we can't just go out for the fun of it?"

I smile. "Of course we can. We can do something next week, just the two of us."

Anna slowly smiles. "Like a date?"

I realize we have never actually gone out for dinner or anything just the two of us. "No, exactly like a date." If it makes Anna happy, I will take her out every week if I have to.

"God, get a room already." Nico slides into the empty chair across the table.

I frown at Nico. "Not having a good night?"

"In less than 5 minutes, it will be a new year but I have the same crappy shit I have to deal with. Gia has been calling and texting me non-stop. She is miserable and wants to make me miserable as well."

Anna turns to me. "Unban Gia. That would fix things."

Nico shakes his head. "Gia is a miserable person. It doesn't matter what you do, it will never be enough." Nico finishes his drink and gets up. "I'm going to find someone to ring in the new year with." Nico walks towards one of the waitresses and he whispers something in her ear. Her face goes red, and she giggles in response. I get why people call him a prince. If I didn't know what he did for a living, I too would think the same.

"I wish there was something we could do about Nico and Gia." Anna pouts.

"Yeah, me too."

There is nothing more I want than my brother to be happy, but he and Gia are married. We do not believe in divorce.

In the beginning, Nico tried everything to make the marriage work, but it was never enough for Gia. She wanted a husband who waited on her hand and foot. When Nico would be at work, she would go nuts saying he wasn't giving her enough attention. When he tried to spend time with her, she said he wasn't trying hard enough.

Eventually, Nico realized it was never going to work and offered Gia a chance to live separate lives. But she refused. I think it was because she hated the thought of Nico being with someone else. She couldn't have him so no one else could either.

Instead, she has trapped him in a miserable marriage and uses every opportunity she has to make his life hard.

Everyone in the bar starts counting down to midnight. "Five, four, three, two, one." Everyone erupts in cheers and screaming happy new year. Streamers and balloons fall from the ceiling.

Anna laughs as a streamer falls on her head. Despite the difficult year she has had, we found a way to work.

Anna turns to me. "Happy new year." Her voice is barely above a whisper.

"Happy new year." I run my hand up her back and she shudders at my touch. I pull her towards me and kiss her. She cups my cheeks with both hands and deepens the kiss.

CHAPTER 40

Anna

T oday is Emma's first ballet lesson. Our SUV pulls up in front of the ballet school and Emma jumps in her seat in excitement.

I help her unbuckle out of her seat and help out of the SUV. Dino comes around, blocking anyone from getting near us.

Once Emma is out, I grab Daniele out of his car seat and put him in his stroller. This is also Daniele's first day out. In the last several weeks he has grown so much.

I grab one hand of Emma's and use the other to steer the stroller and head towards the ballet school. Dino opens the door for me, and I give him a small smile and thank him.

Once inside I find a spot near the back of the large room with one entire wall being a mirror where the lessons are going to take place.

I help Emma out of her jacket and straighten her tutu. I fix her hair into a little bun and hope it stays in place. Emma's hair tends to have a mind of its own.

The ballet instructor, a tall blonde, calls out for all the students to come and form a circle around her.

Emma takes a seat with the other students. The instructor introduces herself as Ashley. She asks the students to follow her as she stretches her body.

Emma follows the lead of Ashley but every so often she turns around to make sure I am still here. I wave at her a few times, so she knows I'm not going anywhere.

After the stretching, the instructor Ashley teaches the students some basic beginner moves. While Ashley is turned away helping another student, a girl with pigtails pushes Emma.

I'm stunned at another child putting their hands on my daughter but hold it in. They are just children, I tell myself.

Emma looks surprised by the push but continues to follow the instructions.

A few minutes later the pigtail girl kicks Emma! I get up from my seat in horror that my child is being hit. I look around to see if anyone else has noticed but most of the parents are either on their phones or talking amongst themselves.

I consider what to do and decide to let it go. I don't want to be that parent that causes a scene on the first day. Daniele starts to cry, and I pick him up from the stroller and as I continue to keep an eye on Emma. Emma does her best to ignore the pigtail girl. The rest of the class goes by without another incident.

Emma rushes towards me at the end of the class. I'm still holding Daniele in my arms, but I crouch down to my knees. "Did you have fun?"

Emma smiles. "I did."

I'm glad she had fun, but I notice her turn slightly towards the direction of the pigtail girl. I decide I should speak to the girl's mother to prevent any further incidents in the future.

"My love, why don't you take a seat here and I will be right back?" I pat the wooden bench next to me. Emma takes a seat on the bench and I get up and head towards the girl's mother.

The girl's mother has short blonde hair and looks to be in her mid-thirties.

"Excuse me," I say politely.

The woman turns around and looks at me confused. "Can I help you?"

"My daughter Emma was in the same lesson as your daughter, and I noticed your daughter pushed and kicked her during the lesson." I try to keep my voice calm and polite.

"And?" the woman says.

I'm thrown off at her lack of reaction. I just told her, her daughter hit my child and she seems to not care one bit.

I swallow down my anger and continue with my calm voice. "And I was hoping you would talk to your daughter, so she won't do that again."

"How about you talk to your daughter and have her grow some balls?" The woman smirks.

I drop my nice act. "Look I will not have your daughter bullying my daughter."

"And what are you going to do about it?" she mocks.

I want to throttle this woman, but I feel Daniele squirm in my arms. I see a shadow come over and the woman's face drops.

"Is everything okay?" I turn towards the familiar voice and see it's Alessio. "Is something wrong?" he asks.

The woman shakes her head. "No, nothing's wrong."

I stare at the woman dumbfounded. "Actually there is something wrong. This woman's daughter hit our daughter twice and she thinks that's okay!"

Her eyes widen in an almost comical way.

"Is that so?" Alessio takes a threatening step forward.

"I will talk to my daughter and make sure she never hits your kid again. I promise," the woman squeaks.

Alessio narrows his eyes. "You make sure of that."

The woman bobbles her head in a nod and grabs her daughter and walks towards the exit.

I turn to Alessio and I can see why people are afraid of him. Despite being unbelievably handsome, he has this dark aura. He scared me in the past but now I know he would never hurt me.

"What are you doing here?"

"I came to see if you wanted to go out for lunch. It might not be the two of us with the kids, but I thought you would still enjoy it." He shrugs in indifference.

I smile at Alessio for taking me out to eat. When he said he would take me out more often on New Year's Eve, I didn't hold on to it.

Him taking the time out of his day and trying melts my heart. "I would love that."

I head back to Emma. "Emma, look. Your daddy came to take us for lunch." Emma peers up and jumps off the bench and runs to Alessio. He scoops her up in one big motion and kisses her on the cheek. I put a now sleeping Daniele into his stroller and grab Emma's jacket from the bench. "Let's go."

Alessio

Anna is cutting pasta for Emma to make it easier to eat. Emma insists she can do it herself but tends to have most of the pasta miss her mouth if not cut.

Once the pasta is cut into bite-size pieces, Emma grabs the fork that looks like it belongs to a giant in her tiny hands and scoops a piece of pasta into her mouth.

Once Emma has swallowed, Anna smiles and pats the top of Emma's head. "That's my girl."

Daniele squirms in his stroller and Anna goes to pick him up.

I motion for her to stop. "I got this. You should eat before your food gets cold." I pick my boy up and cradle him in my arms. Anna smiles at me exhaustingly and picks up her fork and knife.

"I actually wanted to talk to you about something?" I start.

Anna looks up at me with an unsure expression. "About what?"

"I was thinking we should go on a trip as a family."

Anna's eyes go from uneasiness to shining with excitement. "Where were you thinking?"

"Milan, Italy."

Anna squeals. "Really!? I've never been there."

I smile at her excitement. "I have some business I need to deal with there and I thought you and the kids would enjoy it as well."

"When were you thinking?"

"I was thinking about leaving this Friday?"

"I'm so excited. Thank you, Alessio." Anna turns to Emma. "Emma, we are going on a trip!"

Emma looks up with her chin covered in sauce and smiles.

I'm happy Anna and Emma are excited because despite having business in Italy, my true motive for leaving New York City for a couple of days is another reason.

Carter had learned from one of his sources Ronan is back in the city and has hired a hitman to go after Anna. While he and Nico track down the hitman and take him out, I thought it's best Anna and the children are as far away as possible.

CHAPTER 41

Anna

I'm so excited about the trip to Italy. I have been packing the last couple of days for every occasion just to be prepared.

We are about to head out for the airport in an hour when my phone rings. It's an unknown number. I pick it up and wait for the person on the other end to respond.

"Anna, how is my girl doing?" A cold shiver runs down my spine at the voice. Ronan.

I quickly hang up. The phone rings again. I drop it on the bed and just stare at it ringing. Once, twice and a third time.

Alessio walks into the room and sees my face and is instantly alarmed. "What's wrong?" He comes to me and tries to grab my hand, but I flinch and back away. It's like everything I have worked hard to forget is being pushed back to the surface.

Alessio looks hurt by my reaction. "Anna?"

The phone rings again and he picks it up from the bed.

"Don't answer," I stammer out. "It's Ronan."

Alessio's face morphs into anger and he answers the call and puts it to his ear. He doesn't say anything, but I can hear Ronan talking on the other end. I don't know what he is saying but Alessio's face rages with fury.

"Ronan, it's you who I will cut into little pieces and scatter across the city!" Alessio roars on the phone.

He ends the call and slams it against the wall, shattering my phone in to pieces. I flinch at his sudden outburst and step back.

I feel the walls are caving in and the oxygen is being sucked out. I waver and fall to the ground. I try to breathe but I can't seem to get any oxygen in my lungs despite breathing heavily in and out. My head spins with images of Ronan and him making threats to hurt Emma. Him lashing out at me while I protect Daniele in my belly. I try to scratch the images out and I feel my hands being restrained.

"Anna, look at me!" Alessio shouts.

The images clear and I see Alessio in front of me. He has my wrists in his hands and his eyes are filled with sadness. Sadness for me. Tears fall down my cheeks and I can't help but cry.

Alessio pulls me towards him and holds me tight. I cry for not only the pain I suffered at Ronan's hands but for everything I have held in for years.

I let it all out and cry for those I have lost. I cry for those I fought for. I cry for all that I have suffered. I continue to cry until my eyes are all dried up. I don't know how long I cried, but I can feel Alessio's shirt is soaked from my tears. But he doesn't say anything. He just holds me in his arms making me feel safe.

Alessio

When Ronan called, I was furious. When I picked up the call, he didn't realize I was the one on the other end. He taunted Anna and threatened to finish what he started.

I had lost it but tried to reign in my anger until I saw the real damage was already done.

Anna broke in front of my very eyes. She shattered into pieces and succumbed to the pain.

I grabbed her wrists when she started thrashing at her face to prevent her from hurting herself anymore.

Eventually, she let it all out. I held her in my arms and kept telling her "It's okay." I don't think she heard me as she didn't react.

I finally let her go when she fell asleep in my arms. I picked her up and laid her on the bed and covered her in a blanket to keep her warm.

I headed downstairs and called Nico, informing him the trip was off. We couldn't go to Italy in Anna's state. I had Nico increase security around the penthouse for the time being in case Ronan made a move.

I'm watching the city skyline when Daniele wails on the baby monitor. I get back upstairs to his room and pick him up out of his crib, and he stops crying once in my arms.

He peers up at me with his blue eyes, the same as Anna's. He scrunches his nose in annoyance and wails again. It's his feeding time.

I head to the kitchen and luckily there is milk Anna has pumped already in the fridge. She had prepared it for the plane ride to Italy.

I warm it up and test it on my wrist to make sure it's not too hot. I position the bottle towards Daniele who grabs the bottle and starts sucking.

I can't help but notice Daniele is around the same age Emma was when Maria had died. The thought sends a hallowing pain through my heart at losing Anna.

I won't lose Anna.

CHAPTER 42

Anna

I wake up to darkness. I wait for my eyes to adjust to the dark and realize I'm in bed. I lift my head off Alessio's chest and peer over at the clock. It's 4 am in the morning.

I slowly pull out of Alessio's grasp and slide out of bed without making any noise. I tiptoe out of our bedroom and close the door lightly behind me.

I head to Emma's room first and walk in to see her sleeping in her bed with her hair in every direction. I sweep her hair off her face and pull the blanket up to her chest. I kiss her on the head, and she scratches the spot in her sleep and flips over onto her stomach.

I head over to Daniele's room and peer over the crib. He is wide awake. When he sees me, he smiles and kicks his little legs in excitement.

I pick him up and cradle him on my chest. I kiss him on the head and his baby scent fills my nose. My eyes fill with tears. My son's little arms lift up towards me as he lays his head against my chest. I rock him back and forth and sing him a lullaby. His eyes get heavy, and they slowly start to close.

I take a seat on the rocking chair in the corner and continue to hum another lullaby.

Today Ronan broke me. He was able to take me back to that pain I have tried so hard to forget.

I realize now that I can't forget the pain. I can't pretend everything is okay. I need to overcome it by accepting it. I can't give up. I need to continue to fight for my family.

Alessio

My chest feels cool. I can't help but think something is missing. I snap my eyes open and see that Anna is gone. I look around the room and don't see her anywhere.

The last time she disappeared in the middle of the night I found her on the balcony ready to jump. I throw the bed covers to the side and run downstairs hoping I'm not too late.

When I get downstairs it's quiet. I don't see Anna anywhere. My heart drops. What if I'm too late. I walk out on the balcony. My steps feel heavy as I walk towards the end. I look off the balcony and down below and see nothing. I breathe a sigh of relief.

I head back inside and go through each room downstairs from the kitchen to the guest bedroom. My heart starts to race again. What if she went outside? The alarm would have gone off if she did but maybe she found a way around it.

I head back upstairs and check Emma's room first. She's fast asleep in her bed. Then I go to Daniele's room.

I open Daniele's door and find Anna sitting on a rocking chair with Daniele in her arms. The pain in my stomach disappears instantly. "Thank god."

I walk over to her and fall to my knees in front of Anna. I lay my head on her thighs and don't move. I need to feel her. I need reassurance that she is safe and right here.

I feel her hand lightly go through my hair. "I'm sorry," she says lightly.

I feel her legs and up her thighs and grip them. She flinches at the sudden hold. I raise my head and look Anna in the eyes. "Don't ever do that again."

She gives me a small smile. "I don't plan on it." I can't help the emotions that run through me at this moment.

With one arm still wrapped around Daniele, Anna uses her free hand to lightly cup my cheeks. She soothingly rubs her thumb and leans forward and kisses me. The pain and panic within me are replaced with warmth. Anna's warmth.

CHAPTER 43

Alessio

N ico walks into my office and from his face, I can tell it's not good news.

"Did you find any information on Ronan or about the hitman he hired?"

Nico halts in the middle of the room. "According to Carter's sources, Ronan has hired an international hitman to go after Anna."

I pale at Nico's news. Anna seems to have gone back to normal before she received the call from Ronan, but I worry about her. I saw the pain on her face when she was in my arms.

"I'm going to kill every Irishman in this city for what Ronan did to Anna."

Nico nods in understanding. "I promised you I would help you and I meant it. I will do whatever it takes for you to get justice for Anna."

"It won't be easy. The Irish are stronger and more powerful than the Yakuza." When the Yakuza killed my first wife Maria, I had dismantled their entire organization and eradicated them out of the city. But the Irish aren't like the Yakuza. Their reach is wide and will be harder to kill.

Nico smirks. "Like that will stop us."

No, it won't.

Anna

It's Emma's second ballet lesson and she has been excited all morning for it. Today it's just me and Emma. I left Daniele behind with Greta since he seemed a bit cranky today.

We pull up to the ballet school and I look around for the mom and child with whom I previously argued with. To my surprise, they are nowhere to be seen. I can't help but wonder if Alessio's appearance scared them away. None the less, it's better for Emma.

All the other parents are staring in my direction. I'm assuming it has to do with the half dozen guards scattered around us and outside watching the perimeter.

It may seem a bit overkill but with Ronan's sudden reappearance, Alessio said it was needed. I could tell there was more he was keeping from me, but I decided to let it go. I didn't want to know. I'm barely holding on as it is and don't need any more bad news.

Emma is in her pink tutu and as always, during class, she turns to make sure I'm still there every few minutes. I smile and wave at her, giving her the reassurance she needs.

She hasn't said anything about being kidnapped and doesn't seem to have any bad dreams, but I can't help but wonder what goes on in her mind.

She is still young and innocent, and I think for that reason, the horrible and traumatizing incident didn't fully engrave itself into her.

My phone vibrates in my pocket and I pull it out. Unknown number. My heart thumps against my chest. I know it's Ronan. I don't pick it up. A few seconds later I get a text message. With shaking fingers I open the text.

Meet me outside behind the building or I will blow up the entire building with your precious daughter still inside. Warn the guards and I blow it up.

My heart drops. I look around to see if I can see Ronan, but I don't. I consider warning Dino who is standing a few feet away from me, but I risk hurting Emma.

In that moment I make my choice.

I push up from the bench and walk over to Dino and smile. "I'm going to the washroom. Please take care of Emma for me."

Dino nods in acknowledgment.

I walk over to the washroom in the corner and once inside I look around. I see a small window and decide that's my way out.

I grab the trash can and flip it over and use it as a stepping stool. I wiggle my way out of the window and fall to my knees on the cement street outside. The thick layer of my jeans protects my skin from getting scratched up.

A pair of shoes come into view, and I look up to see it's Ronan.

"Hello, Anna." Ronan's fist comes towards me, and everything goes dark.

Alessio

"We need to kill him now!" I roar at my brothers.

Carter shakes his head. "We don't know where he is and even if we did it won't be that easy. I'm sure he has taken measures to protect himself."

It's been days and no news of Ronan. I'm getting impatient at the lack of progress we have made.

My phone rings and I answer it without even looking at the caller's name. "What?" I bark.

There's a pause for a second. "Boss, I'm sorry." It's Dino.

"Sorry for what?" I ask hesitantly.

"Anna is gone. She said she was going to the washroom and never returned. When we went in to look for her, we found it empty."

My heart stops beating. "What about Emma?"

"We have her."

Emma's safe. But Anna is gone.

"Take Emma to the penthouse. I'm on my way." I hang up the call. Nico and Carter are waiting for me to fill them in. "Anna is gone. Dino has Emma and is taking her back to the penthouse."

"Gone?" Carter questions. "How can she just be gone?"

I start my laptop and pull up the website for Anna's tracker. Only the password is incorrect. "What the hell?"

Nico comes around my desk and peers over my shoulder. "Did you change the password?"

"No."

"It must have been Anna's brothers," Carter points out.

Of course. They wanted Anna back home. Maybe they found a way to finally get to her. I rise from my seat. "I'm going to go meet Nikolai Petrov."

"We are coming with you," Nico says.

I shake my head. "Not you." I swallow the lump forming in my throat. "If something happens to me, you will have to take over. Not to mention take care of Emma and Daniele."

"Nothing is going to happen to you," Nico reassures me.

"Still. I need you here. Carter can come with me."

Nico is about to argue but then stops and nods. As much as he hates it, he knows this is the right thing to do. If Nikolai does have Anna, us showing up could end with us being dead.

CHAPTER 44

Alessio

C arter and I pull up in front of the Petrov estate. We get out and as usual, Dima meets us at the door. "What are you doing here?"

I stand firm. "We are here to talk to your boss Nikolai."

"About what?"

"This is between me and Nikolai."

"Wait here." Dima heads back inside and then returns a few minutes later. "Follow me."

Carter and I follow Dima inside to Yuri's old office, now Nikolai's.

Once inside, Nikolai and Maxim stand from their seats. Maxim being expressionless as usual doesn't say a thing.

Nikolai crosses his arm. "Why are you here?"

I try to hold in my anger, not giving Nikolai the benefit of thinking he has won. "You know why? I'm here for Anna."

Nikolai nods. "I was going to contact you. Anna insists on staying married to you so I think we should renegotiate the alliance between our two families."

"Is that why you took Anna?" My voice is calm, but my hands shake with anger. I fist my hands to hide it.

Nikolai uncrosses his arms and is alarmed. "What do you mean take? Did something happen to Anna?"

Maxim's eyes have shifted from expressionless to something else.

"I thought you took Anna? She is missing. Her bracelet tracker password was changed."

Nikolai walks back to his desk and starts inputting information in his laptop with Maxim hovering nearby. "I changed the password in case Anna decided she wanted to leave your ass. I didn't want you to have a way to track her."

I walk over to Nikolai's laptop and see that the tracker is saying Anna is back in the building she was previously kidnapped to. I turn to Carter. "Let's go. Ronan has her."

"We are coming too," Nikolai announces. "She is our sister. Don't try to stop us, it won't work."

I nod. "Okay." We could use all the help we can get.

CHAPTER 45

Anna

I wake up to a throbbing pain on the side of my head, near my right eye. I feel it gently and it feels soft and painful.

I groan at the pain and force myself to straighten. I look around the room and realize I'm back in the same place Ronan had kept me before.

The same hell. I feel the mental walls forming again. I push back against the wall in an attempt to put distance, but I have nowhere to go. I'm trapped.

The door flies open and Ronan walks in proudly and victorious. "Anna, you are awake."

I don't respond.

"We never got to finish our little game last time."

I still don't answer.

"Are you ready to begin where we left off?"

I give him my silence. Last time he had Emma to use and force his hand. This time Emma is safe with Dino and he can't hold someone I love over me.

The smile Ronan has drops when I don't respond. He walks over to me and pulls me up by my hair.

It's an excruciating pain but I don't make a sound. I won't let him win again.

"Don't want to talk, huh?" Ronan smiles like a wolf. "Let's see how long that lasts." He pulls me by my hair out the door and down the hall and into another room where he lets me go. I fall down onto my hands and knees. I recognize the room again. It is where Ronan had tortured me last time.

Ronan licks his lips. "Which level are we on again? Oh, right level four."

Ronan turns to grab something from the table at the side and I can't help but burst out laughing.

He turns to me and looks stunned and then confused. "What's so funny?"

I don't answer but continue to laugh. His eyes rage with anger at my laughing fit but I can't help it. I'm not laughing because the situation is funny but because of how ridiculous this is. I am back at the same place I tried so hard to forget. I was so afraid to be back here but now that I am, I realize I give it too much power over me.

I decide to taunt him, despite knowing it would probably make things worse. "I'm laughing because you are so pathetic. You tried to break me once, but you failed. And now you have taken me again thinking you have won but like before you will fail again," I taunt. I won't let him win so easily. I rise to my feet. "Go ahead, Ronan, give it your best shot."

Ronan storms towards me like a ball of fury and I'm waiting for his hit when suddenly an explosion goes off. A round of shots can be heard from a distance.

Ronan pulls out his gun and grabs me by the arm. "You're coming with me."

He pulls me out and starts dragging me down the hallway. I try and pull my arm out of his hold, but he tightens it further to the point I lose blood circulation. We go through a door and are outside when the night cold air hits my face. The bruise on my face feels even more sensitive from the sudden temperature change.

Alessio appears from around the corner. "Stop!"

Ronan pulls me towards him as a shield and cocks his gun to my forehead. "Unless you want your wife's pretty little brains to splatter all over, I would drop the gun, Vitale."

Alessio doesn't lower his gun and I see one of the Italian soldiers coming around the other corner. When he nears us, all of a sudden, the soldier falls to the ground with a bullet hole in the middle of his head.

Ronan tsks. "Did you think I would not come prepared? I have a highly skilled hitman ready to take you all out. Drop the gun or I have him shoot you in the head next."

"No!" I scream. The thought of Alessio dying is unbearable.

Ronan laughs but Alessio doesn't waver. He holds his gun steady on Ronan.

"I warned you," Ronan says.

Then I hear a whistling sound from the distance of a gunshot going off, but Alessio is still standing.

Alessio smiles. "Your hitman has been taken out."

Ronan drops his smile realizing he is trapped. He starts to move back and with his grip on me, I'm being pulled with him. We are nearing a dock and the water.

"Let Anna go," Alessio warns.

"Fine, catch!" Ronan pushes me forward towards Alessio and I hear a splash behind me.

Alessio catches me in his arms. "Are you okay?"

I nod and turn behind me to see where Ronan is.

"Stay here." Alessio motions for me to stay put. He walks over to the edge of the dock and crouches down. He shakes his head. "Dammit, he's gone." He walks back to me. He gently touches the bruise on my face from being punched and I flinch out of pain.

A few seconds later, Carter and my brother Nikolai walk out of the warehouse.

"Nikolai, what are you doing here?" I ask my brother.

Nikolai shrugs. "I found out my sister was taken. Thought I'd join in the fun." His voice is of indifference, but I know it's an act. He is pretending not to care. He's done this since we were little so others would not see how much he cares for me. He didn't want others like my papa to use me as a way to hurt him.

I smile and walk over to him and give him a hug. "Thank you." I see his hand twitch to hug me back but he doesn't move. "Where is Maxim?" I ask.

"Up top." Nikolai juts his chin in the direction of one of the rooftops of a building. I realize it was Maxim who shot the hitman earlier. He was always good with his shots. He never missed and was always precise.

Alessio comes from behind and puts an arm around my waist and pulls me back. "We should get you checked out back home."

"We will stay back here," Nikolai says. "I'm going to have my team comb the waters for Ronan."

"I'll stay back as well," Carter declares.

Alessio nods and grabs my hand to drag me away. "Let's go home."

CHAPTER 46

Anna

As soon as I enter the penthouse, Emma runs right at me, almost knocking me down despite her small stature.

I kneel down and give her a hug and I feel her small body shake in my arms. I pull away to get a better look at her face. "What's wrong, my love?" I ask.

Emma sniffles. "You left me."

The pain in Emma's voice sends a stab in my heart. "I'm sorry, I will never leave you again."

Emma's face is covered in tears and snot. "Promise? You never break a promise."

I push Emma's hair off her face. "Promise."

Emma wraps her small hands around my neck and cries into the crook of my neck. I gently stroke her back and let her cry her pain away.

After a few minutes, Greta steps forward. "Emma, now that is enough. Your mom didn't leave you and never will. Come now, it's time for bed." She holds out her hand for Emma to grab.

Emma peels herself away from me and goes to grab Greta's hand but turns around to look at me.

"I'm not going anywhere," I reassure her.

She gives a small nod and takes Greta's hand who leads her upstairs for bed.

I straighten and see Dino standing in the corner.

"I'm sorry, Mrs. Vitale, I won't let you out of my sight again. I don't know how this happened," Dino staggers out.

I raise my hand and give him a small smile. "It's okay, it's not your fault."

"No, it's not," Alessio says firmly with a hint of anger from behind me.

Dino must sense it as well, as he excuses himself right away.

Once it is only the two of us, I turn to Alessio. "I know you're mad," I start, "but I did what I had to do to protect Emma. Ronan was threatening to blow up the building with Emma inside if I didn't meet him."

"And what about you?" Alessio intrudes in my explanation.

"What about me?"

"You decided to just run into Ronan's hands knowing he will torture and probably kill you without thinking?" Alessio's voice sounds calm and relaxed, but I can see the rage in his eyes. He is holding it in.

"I was thinking of Emma," I say slowly, trying not to trigger Alessio's anger.

Alessio's fists clench and I take a step back. "Alessio," I say lightly.

He looks at me for a few seconds and then his face softens. He sighs "I almost lost you." Slowly Alessio's face transforms to dread and pain. I take a step forward and lightly touch his cheek. "But you didn't."

"Only because of that damn bracelet. But next time –" His voice breaks.

I know what he is thinking, and I want to tell him there won't be a next time, but I can't. We don't know that. Ronan is still out there and even if he's not, there is always going to be another Ronan.

I go on my tiptoes and give Alessio a light kiss. He closes his eyes and relaxes. "Let's not think about that. Let's go to bed." I grab Alessio's hand and lead him upstairs.

Alessio

Anna is safe for now, but I can't stop thinking about the future. Ronan is a threat. Anna and the kids are asleep.

I take the elevator down to Carter's penthouse. Once I get there, I see Carter and Nico sitting on the couch. They both turn when I walk in.

"Did you find Ronan?" I ask Carter.

Carter shakes his head, "He's gone. I'm sorry."

I release the anger that I have been holding in. I grab the glass tumblers at the bar and throw them at the wall. One after another until my anger subsides.

"I will get justice for you and your family," Nico says. "Give me time. I will find him and make him pay for what he has done."

I grab the now-only bottle of alcohol on the bar and take a seat on the couch. I unscrew the top and drink straight from the bottle. The liquor burns down my throat in an almost painful way.

I face Nico. "You made a promise to bring Ronan to me. I need you to keep it. As long as he is out there, Anna is not safe."

Nico grabs the bottle out of my hand and angles his head back and takes a mouthful. "And I will keep that promise. At any cost."

Carter now grabs the bottle from Nico and follows his lead. "Same. I will do whatever it takes as well."

I know I can rest knowing my brothers will keep their promise and bring Ronan to his demise.

CHAPTER 47

Five months later

Alessio

Things have been going well for the last couple of months. The Vitale Family and the Petrov Family re-formed the alliance.

After Anna's second kidnapping, Nikolai approached us and offered an alliance that is beneficial and fair to both parties.

Nico was hesitant once again of the Russians, but Nikolai and Maxim seem to care about Anna. More than her father ever did. In the end, we made it work. They have supported us in our efforts to find Ronan and we have helped them expand their drug routes.

It's Mother's Day and Emma had woken us up early this morning in excitement. Even more than she was during Christmas.

They are currently at a beauty spa that Anna had planned for her and Emma to spend time together.

Daniele is playing on a blanket in the middle of my home office with an annoying toy that makes animal sounds. I want to throw it out of the window, but he smiles every time it makes that irritating noise.

Nico barges into my office and halts when he sees Daniele. He goes down on his hunches and tickles my son who gives him a toothless grin.

Once he straightens and makes eye contact with me, his face shifts. I know it's not good news.

I get up from my seat and head towards Daniele and pick him up into my arms. "I can tell something is wrong. What is it?"

"Depends how you look at it," Nico dodges my question.

Daniele grabs my chin and smiles up at me. My heart melts every time I see him like this. I know one day I will have to prepare him to be Capo but for now, I will protect him, Emma, and Anna.

Nico clears his throat. "Our alliance with Petrov is starting to pay off. Nikolai was able to find Ronan." Before I can even ask where Nico resumes, "He was in Chicago a few days ago, meeting with the Mancini Family."

"Don't tell me he forged an alliance with them."

Nico nods. "He did. Similar to ours with the Russians. Ronan will marry Lorenzo Mancini's daughter, Lily, forging the two families." Fuck this is bad. The Mancinis are a powerful family, and their involvement complicates things.

"What do they get out of this?" I ask Nico.

"No idea but I'm going to take care of this." Nico smirks. "I got a plan."

Anna

I return home with Emma from our little spa day. She woke up before dawn in pure excitement and now is feeling the side effect of waking up so early. She rubs her sleepy eyes as we walk into the penthouse.

"My love, how about a nap?"

Emma's face is filled with exhaustion, but she haphazardly shakes her head. "No sleep. It's Mother's Day."

"We can continue Mother's Day once you wake up from your nap." I try to coerce her into sleeping.

I can tell she wants to argue but the tiredness is weighing on her. She finally caves. "Okay."

I lead her to her bedroom and help her into her frilly pink pajamas and tuck her into bed. She gives me a smile before falling asleep. I kiss the top of her forehead and close the door.

Once I get downstairs, I head straight to Alessio's office to check in on him and Daniele.

Despite his busy work schedule, he volunteered to work from home to watch Daniele.

I knock on his office door gently and pop my head in. Alessio seemed to be in a deep conversation with Nico which I have now interrupted as they turn to face me. "I'm sorry, am I intruding?"

Alessio smiles. "No, you're not, come in. Nico was just leaving." Daniele smiles and flays in Alessio's arm in excitement to see me. I head over to Alessio and stick out my hands for Alessio to pass Daniele over to me, which he does. I kiss Daniele's cheek and he grins widely at me.

I turn to greet Nico who I notice was staring at Daniele in almost longing.

He and Gia don't have any kids which is probably for the best considering how toxic their relationship is. I can't help but feel sorry for Nico. He is great with Emma and Daniele, and I can tell he wants children of his own.

Nico gives me an almost sad smile. "I should go."

"Why don't you and Carter come for dinner tonight? I can cook pasta," I volunteer.

Nico is surprised at my invitation and his smile grows. "I will let Carter know. I should get back to work. See you tonight then."

I nod and smile at Nico as he exits.

Alessio gently touches my hip. "That was unexpected."

"I know. I just feel so sad for Nico and Carter. They both seem so unhappy sometimes. I wish there was something more I could do than make dinner."

Alessio kisses the top of my head. "I love that you care about my brothers."

Now it's my turn to give a sad smile. Alessio has said he loves a lot of things about me but has never once said he *loves* me.

I know it's hypocritical of me to want Alessio to say he loves me when I have never said it. But the truth is I am scared. I realized how much I love Alessio when Ronan kidnapped me a second time, but I have been too much of a coward to say it.

I have faced a lot of horrible and painful things but telling Alessio I love him and not hearing it back might be the most painful. It would cut my heart into pieces.

Daniele pulls at my hair to get my attention. I warn him with a finger for grabbing my hair and then give him the attention he has been seeking. "Are you hungry?"

Daniele, unable to talk, gives me his beautiful smile. For a baby, he has the most charming smile I have ever seen. I already know it's going to break a lot of girls' hearts when he gets older. I give Alessio a quick peck on the lips and leave his office to feed my son.

Emma is sitting at the dining table pouting. When she woke up from her nap and found me cooking, she wasn't happy, stating it's Mother's Day and I shouldn't be working.

Alessio, Nico, and Carter have already taken their seats around the table with their wine. I walk over to the table and put down the bruschetta for the appetizer.

I have been learning different Italian recipes for the last several months. Even Greta was impressed at my progress.

I walk over to Emma's chair and give her a kiss on the top of her head to ease her anger. She melts at my contact and gives a small smile. When she notices Alessio staring she quickly crosses her arm and goes back to pouting.

I grab the mushroom risotto and chicken parmigiana and bring it back to the table and place it down and take a seat to the right of Alessio.

"This looks great," Nico says while filling up his plate.

"I'm glad. Greta's been teaching me to cook Italian dishes but I'm still learning."

"Mommy is a good cook," Emma proudly declares. I smile at my beautiful daughter and smooth out her unruly brown hair. She peers up at me with a mouthful of chicken and grins.

"Do you guys have any plans for the summer?" Carter asks slowly while making eye contact with Alessio.

"No."

Alessio clears his throat. "Actually I was thinking we finally take that trip to Italy."

My eyes widen in excitement. "When were you thinking?"

Alessio shrugs. "I was thinking maybe next month."

"Oh, that would be amazing!" I smack my hands together in excitement.

I need to start planning now. Make a list of things we need to take, especially with the kids. I don't miss the look Alessio gives Nico and Carter. They're up to something but I don't care. I'm just so happy to be able to go on a vacation.

CHAPTER 48

Alessio

It's the day we are leaving for Italy. Anna has been up since four in the morning packing last-minute things.

She has packed everything from clothes to toys for the kids. Whenever I think she is done packing she remembers another thing the kids might need.

Considering their young age, they need a lot of things.

Daniele has just started drinking formula which we have to pack in case we can't find the same brand in Italy. And then Emma insists on taking her ballet outfits with her.

While Anna is finishing up packing upstairs, I decided to finish some work in my home office before the flight.

I plan on working while in Italy but most of the heavy lifting will have to be done by Nico and Carter in my place.

Nico barges in just as I'm finishing up. I close my laptop and lean back in my chair. "You only have a month."

"I know." Nico nods. "I won't let you down. When I'm done Ronan won't be able to hurt you or your family."

This sudden trip to Italy was not planned for vacation purposes. Like before, it was planned to get my family out of the city while Nico takes care of Ronan.

"I don't want him dead. I want him alive when I return. He is mine to kill." The anger surges through me as I recall all the horrible things Ronan has done to my family.

"Don't worry I'll be sure to keep him alive long enough for you to finish him off," Nico smirks.

I hear a light knock on the door, and I know instantly it's Anna. Only she would knock so gently.

The door opens and Anna pops her head in. "I'm done packing and ready to go. But if you have some work to do, I can wait."

I shake my head. "Nico just came to say goodbye."

Anna fully opens the door and walks in. She is wearing a tight white t-shirt and denim shorts, while her golden wavy hair is cascading down her back.

But my eyes are focused on her legs; they look long and lean with the strappy heels she is wearing.

"I'm sure Emma will be happy to see you before we leave."

"Where is the little ballerina?" Nico asks.

Anna smiles. "Upstairs packing her ballet books. I'll go bring her and Daniele so they can say goodbye." Anna turns and leaves to get the kids.

I get up from my chair. "One month," I remind Nico.

Nico grins. "Don't worry."

But I can't help but worry. As long as Ronan is out there, I can't rest. I need him in front of me so I can shred him piece by piece for what he has done.

Nico and I head back into the living room where Anna brings Emma and Daniele downstairs. Emma runs straight into Nico's arms and begins telling him about how excited she is for the trip. Daniele on the other hand, who is on Anna's hip, looks like he is ready to fall asleep.

Nico gives Emma a kiss. "I'm going to miss my little ballerina."

Emma grins. "I'm going to miss you too."

Despite going for only a month, it is a month I will be away from my brothers. That's the longest we have ever been away from each other.

Nico places Emma down on the ground and then goes to pick up Daniele. Sleepy Daniele goes to Nico but as soon as he is in Nico's arms, he wraps his arms around

Nico's neck and lays his head on Nico's shoulder and closes his eyes.

I can tell that physical contact with my son has affected Nico. His eyes shift in sadness, but he quickly cloaks them.

When he thinks no one is looking, I notice him looking at Emma and Daniele in longing. I know he would be a great father even with Gia as a mother. But Gia, being the selfish witch that she is, has made it clear she would not ruin her body for a child.

Nico hands my sleeping son to me. "I should get back to work. I will see you in a month." I nod to Nico in acknowledgment.

He gives Anna a goodbye hug and heads out to start what he promised me.

Anna

Thankfully we are flying private, because as soon as we took off, Daniele started screaming bloody murder.

Emma is sitting in a chair across from me on the plane holding her ears closed with her hands.

This is the first time for both of them on a plane and the ears popping from the high altitude is too much for my precious children to handle.

Emma is trying to hold it in, but I can see water forming in her eyes.

Alessio, who was working in the back in a small closed-off section for private meetings on the private plane, heads towards us. He must have heard Daniele's screeching screams all the way in the back.

I smile at him apologetically. "I'm sorry."

He shakes his head. "Don't be." He motions for me to hand Daniele to him and I do. Alessio takes a seat next to me and tries to speak to our son gently.

I pull out my bag from under the seat and take out two sets of noise-canceling headphones. I lean over and put a pair on Emma who is shocked at the sudden silence of the plane. Then I put the other pair on Daniele, hoping it would be enough to soothe him.

After a few minutes, his cries become quieter until he finally looks up with blurry blue eyes with confusion.

I lean down and give his little nose a kiss. He scrunches up his nose, not understanding what is happening.

I stick out my hand. "Here, I can take Daniele if you need to get back to work."

Alessio hands Daniele back to me. "If you or the kids need to rest, there is a bedroom for you to sleep in. It's going to be a couple of hours before we land."

I give Alessio a smile. "We will be fine."

Alessio thins his lips. "I will check up on you in a few hours."

He gets up and heads back to work. I wanted to reassure Alessio we are on a plane, and we will be fine, but he seems to constantly be worried about me and the kids.

I can't blame him with everything that has happened and Ronan still being out there somewhere.

I look down at Emma and see that she still has her bracelet on her. A small comfort knowing we will also be able to find her.

Alessio

We arrived early in the morning in Milan, Italy. Anna didn't sleep a wink on the plane. She was constantly taking care of Emma and Daniele. Despite my suggestions that she rest while I take over, she refused.

We get into the waiting town car at the airport and as soon as we close the door, Anna has fallen asleep with Daniele in her arms.

Emma on the other hand is wide awake after sleeping for several hours on the plane. Once the car is in motion Emma crawls from the middle seat into my lap and peers out of the window in excitement.

When the car comes to a stop at our home in Italy, Anna jerks awake and looks around in confusion. "Where are we?"

"Mommy, we are in Italy!" Emma jumps in excitement in my lap.

The driver opens my door and I get out first. I look back to make sure the security detail is in place. Once I confirm, I help Emma out before helping Anna and Daniele out of the car.

Our home is on a private piece of land surrounded by large gates and security cameras. I had one of my men come out a week earlier to prep security and make sure the security is up to date.

I wasn't going to take any chances with my family.

The house itself is a ten-bedroom yellow-painted villa.

Anna walks in and her eyes glow. "Wow, it's beautiful."

The housekeeper, an older woman, greets us at the door. "Hello, my name is Martha. If you need anything, I am here to help, please let me know. But for now, I can show you to your rooms. You are probably very tired from your journey."

Anna smiles warmly at Martha. "You can call me Anna. And rest sounds good right now."

Martha shows us to our bedrooms while one of the guards brings our luggage inside.

Martha volunteers to help Emma get dressed for bed while we get settled into our room.

I shower and change in our attached bathroom and find Anna passed out in bed with Daniele asleep next to her in the middle of the bed.

I walk over to the bed and pick Daniele up who squirms for a second before falling back asleep and put him in his bassinet.

Despite Daniele's room being set up with a crib, Anna insisted on having him in our bedroom in case he wakes up at night.

I shut off the light and head towards Emma's room who is also asleep. After all the energy she had earlier, she finally exhausted herself and went to bed.

I go back to my bedroom and find Anna leaning over Daniele's bassinet. She turns around in a frenzy until she sees me and settles down.

"I put him in his bassinet so we could sleep."

Anna nods. "Let's sleep." She smiles but I see the worry in her eyes. Anna walks towards the bed, but I block her path. "What's wrong?"

Anna goes rigid. "Nothing."

"Don't lie to me. I thought we had an agreement that we wouldn't keep secrets from each other."

Anna crosses her arms and frowns. "But you're keeping secrets from me. You think I don't know this trip isn't just a random vacation."

I should have known Anna would have figured it out. She's smart and intuitive. I put my hands on Anna's shoulder. "No, it's not a random vacation. I didn't tell you because I didn't want to worry you."

"Worry me about what?" Anna's beautiful face fills with worry, which is why I wanted to keep this from her. "Alessio," she pleads.

"Nico has a lead on Ronan and has a plan to deal with him."

Anna's face pales. "Is he back in the city?"

"We think he was always in the city. Just hiding. But we have a lead now. I don't want you to worry about this."

Anna slowly nods. "So this is why we are here."

"Yes, and I have business here I need to deal with."

"What kind of business?"

I hesitate to tell Anna too much detail about the business, but we did agree to not keep secrets. "The Morelli family who is known for manufacturing the most dangerous and up-to-date weapons reside here. I was hoping to meet with them in hopes of securing a contract for the family. Also wishing we could have a family vacation at the same time."

Anna smiles. "Well I am happy about the vacation part."

"Now it's your turn. Why were you worried earlier?"

Anna drops her smile and looks down.

I grab her chin with my finger and tip her head up. "Anna," I warn.

Anna sighs. "When I woke up and didn't see Daniele, I got scared. I thought he may have been taken. We don't have a bracelet as we do with Emma on him."

Realization washes over me. Her need to constantly be with Daniele and at times even Emma is out of fear. Back home she barely lets Daniele out of her sight when they go out. Even on the plane she refused to sleep because she needed to watch Daniele and Emma.

I take a seat on the bed and pull Anna towards me. She stands in between my legs. "I know it sounds crazy," she says softly.

"No, it doesn't. I worry too but I have taken every precaution there is to make sure nothing happens to the children or you again. I need you to trust me and let me take care of this." I pause and look into Anna's beautiful blue eyes. "You do trust me?"

Anna smiles and puts her arms around my neck and takes a seat on my lap. "Of course I trust you."

Sometimes I don't believe this is real, she's not real. Someone so pure yet strong.

I lightly cup her face to have some contact and she leans down and gives me a kiss. As I deepen the kiss and pull her towards me Daniele sends out a wailing cry.

Anna pulls away but not before giving me another small kiss and walks over to Daniele's bassinet to pick him up. "It's okay," she lulls Daniele in her arms.

The next several days are spent with Anna, Emma, and Daniele going sightseeing while I worked.

I had hoped to meet the Morellis but was told they are no longer in Italy. Their office assistant was vague with the details and refused to provide any details on how to get in touch.

Nico has also put in motion his plan to trap Ronan.

I walk out into the backyard and find Anna with Emma and Daniele picking flowers in the garden. Well, Anna and Emma are picking, while Daniele is sitting on a blanket scrunching the flowers in his fist and destroying them.

"Mommy, Daniele ruined another flower," Emma tattles.

Anna frowns and looks down at Daniele who has a flower squished in between his hands and gives a toothless smile.

"It's okay, my love. I think we have enough flowers." Anna softly pats down Emma's hair, who peers up at her with a smile.

Anna is gentle and kind with everyone, including my children. She doesn't realize it, but she is extraordinarily beautiful. Her father was willing to trade her for power, but he had no idea that Anna was priceless. Even a king's ransom would not be enough.

When I pulled up her veil on our wedding day a year ago, I was captivated by her beauty, but it was her heart and strength that made me fall for her.

Emma gathers the flowers she has and puts them in a large basket almost her size. She tries to carry it but stumbles, dropping the basket of flowers. I pick up the basket for her, "Here mia cara, let me help."

Emma looks up at me and smiles. "Okay."

"What are these for?"

Anna looks up and flashes a sad smile. "Just for fun."

"Here I thought it was for your birthday."

Anna's eyes widen slightly. "You remembered?"

I can't help but laugh. "Of course. You thought I forgot? I'm not that clueless."

Anna picks Daniele up and places him on her waist. "I'm sorry. You have just been so busy, I didn't think you would remember such a small thing."

We start walking back towards the house. "Well I made plans for us to go out to dinner. Martha will watch the kids."

Anna suddenly halts. "You made plans?"

"Don't sound so surprised," I tease.

Anna smiles widely. "So where are we going?"

"That is a surprise."

CHAPTER 49

Anna

I was surprised that Alessio had planned a dinner for us tonight. I was sure he forgot my birthday.

No one besides my brothers really remembered, even then it was not ever celebrated.

After all, having a daughter was not something to celebrate for my papa.

My brothers did send me text messages this morning wishing me a happy birthday, but it just reminded me how much I missed them. I have seen them a handful of times in the last several months now that the two families have renewed the alliance, but they are still cautious.

Over time I hope for it to get better. I miss my brothers a lot.

Alessio didn't tell me where we were going, so I decided to wear a simple white dress and heels. I walk downstairs to meet him and he gives me a kiss on the cheek as soon as he notices me.

Such a small action can melt my heart. Alessio doesn't know it, but he has healed me in so many ways. He thinks I don't trust him, but I trust him completely. Someone like me doesn't open easily to anyone.

"Let's go." Alessio guides me towards the door.

I look back to see Emma standing in the living room door frame waving goodbye. I smile and wave back to her.

Once outside the summer air feels cool on my skin. The driver opens the car door for me, and I get in with Alessio getting in next to me.

I can't help the excitement I feel. Even if Alessio took me to some run-down alley to eat at a hotdog stand I would be happy.

After thirty minutes of driving, we reach a fancy hotel. I get out and look up at the exquisite building.

Alessio puts his arm around me and leads me inside. As soon as we enter, we are greeted by a kind gentleman who takes us towards an elevator.

I lose track of how high we are taken before the elevator doors swing open to a beautiful restaurant.

The gentleman escorts us through the restaurant until we arrive at a closed-off balcony overlooking the city. I am lost for words at how beautiful the night view of Milan is.

Alessio holds out my chair for me and I take a seat. He takes a seat across from me and a waiter arrives within seconds to take our orders. I'm unprepared to order and look at Alessio who places an order for the both of us along with a bottle of wine.

I look out at the view in awe. "The view is so beautiful."

"I think you are more beautiful," Alessio says. I turn towards him and feel my face turning red under Alessio's gaze. He is always showering with compliments. I'm not used to it considering I've always been looked down at.

The waiter brings out the first appetizer and wine. I take a sip of the wine as soon as the waiter hands me the glass.

As soon as the waiter leaves, I can't help but feel shy all of a sudden with only the two of us. Not sure if it's the wine or the sudden surprise dinner but I feel like a little teenager out on her first date.

I clear my throat. "Thank you for this."

Alessio gives me a charming smile. "You're welcome."

The rest of the dinner is spent talking about how Italy is and what I want to do in the next couple of days.

Once dinner is over and Alessio has paid the bill I get up from my seat, the wine hitting me now. I feel wobbly on my feet but try to stand still.

Alessio comes around the table and holds me by the waist. I'm thankful for the support as I would hate to fall and embarrass myself now after such a great evening.

Once we exit the hotel, I look up at the night sky. It's beautiful.

"Can we walk for a bit?" I ask Alessio.

Alessio nods and motions for the driver to wait.

We start walking down the street and under the moonlight; the brick roads and streetlamps look magical. "I love Italy. I hope we can come here again in the future."

"We can if you want."

I turn to Alessio and give him a hug, "thank you for everything. You don't know how much this means to me." I feel my chest getting heavy with emotions and all he has done for me. I'm getting way too emotional.

Alessio pulls away and for some reason, the loss of him feels cold. I look up at my handsome husband who has given me everything I didn't know I needed.

Alessio cups my face. "I'm sorry for everything you have gone through because of me. I will never let you feel pain again. This I promise you. I didn't know how much you meant to me until you were taken but I want you to know I love you and I will do whatever it takes to make you happy."

My heart is racing and feels like it is about to explode into a million pieces. Alessio said he loves me.

I smile at his confession. "I love you too." I wrap my arms around Alessio's neck. I don't want to forget this moment or feeling. I tilt my head up at Alessio and he smiles and leans down and gives me a kiss. His hands are in my hair, and I tug him closer to me to deepen the kiss. His warmth sends a shiver down my spine.

He pulls back and chuckles under his breath, "Let's go home, the children are probably waiting."

I smile at the mention of the children. "Yes, let's go home."

Printed in Great Britain
by Amazon

17763849R00172